FIRST CASE

MURDER ALLEY

ROGER STELLJES

FIRST CASE - Murder Alley

McRyan Mystery Series

By Roger Stelljes

Copyright © 2012 Roger Stelljes

Published by Roger Stelljes

ISBN 9780983575801 (ebook)

ISBN 9781698118079 (paperback)

Enjoying the McRyan Mystery Series?
SILENCED GIRLS (FBI Agent Tori Hunter) is a new series with all new characters.

Never miss a new release again, join the new release list at www. RogerStelljes.com

THE START

O liver walked out of the back of the bar, alone, a rarity for him. Gordon Oliver was a closer.

He didn't fail often.

Yet, tonight he had.

He'd spent the better part of three hours and sixty dollars working a pretty brunette, Natalie. Going deep into his bag of tricks using all of the tools in his toolbox, but he couldn't reel her all the way in. But that was for tonight. Natalie was a semi-regular at The Mahogany and she was interested in him. After all he was leaving with her number and business card. However, for tonight any way, that was all she was giving up.

Gordon smiled to himself. Sometimes having to work for it made it all the more worthwhile when the deal was finally closed. And if past was prologue, he'd close the deal with Natalie soon enough.

He approached his Ford F-150 and reached in his suit pocket for his keys when he heard rustling behind him. He turned, looked towards the big dumpster and sighed, "What are you doing here?"

"Gordon we need to talk."

"I told you I'm done talking about this. You know what you have to do."

"Gordy, I can't right now. I just can't. I need a little more time to deal with him."

Gordon shook his head and turned to walk away, saying: "I can't wait for you to deal with him any longer. I'm sorry, you're out of time."

Those were the last words Gordon Oliver ever uttered.

1

"THIS WASN'T RANDOM."

"I'll take a large Morning Jolt and a medium Dark Roast," Michael McKenzie "Mac" McRyan said to the barista working the counter at The Grand Brew. His purchase would accomplish two things. First, the coffee would get him going as he headed to his first homicide crime scene as a detective. Second, the purchase made him a little money, as he owned part of the coffee shop and twenty others like it with some childhood friends. Mac handed over six dollars, left the change and had the coffees placed into a cardboard carrier. He walked out the front door and climbed into his Explorer and handed a cup to his partner.

"Thanks, partner," Richard Lich, better known as "Dick Lick," said as he set the coffee into the cup holder.

"My pleasure," Mac answered.

McRyan put his Explorer into gear and motored east on Grand towards downtown St. Paul. "So what do we have?" Mac asked.

"Body in an alley behind The Mahogany," Lich answered. "Beyond that I don't know much."

"A murder behind the competition, that should make Shamus happy," Mac said. Shamus was Mac's uncle and he ran the other family business, McRyan's Pub, which sat on the southwestern edge of downtown St. Paul. The Mahogany was a pub on the eastern side of downtown. The two bars catered to different crowds, however. McRyan's Pub catered to cops and hockey fans. The Mahogany was known as the lawyer bar.

As he drove towards downtown and The Mahogany, Mac thought about working his first crime scene as a detective. Being a cop was the first McRyan family business and Mac was part of the fourth generation of McRyan cops. He had numerous uncles and cousins currently in the department and a few retired uncles, who instead of patrolling the streets, now patrolled the bottles and taps behind the brass rail at McRyan's Pub, which was the second McRyan family business.

More significantly, Mac was the son of Simon McRyan, perhaps the best detective ever to walk behind a St. Paul badge.

Because of that, it was not Mac's original plan to be a cop.

When he was a kid, being a cop was what he wanted to be, it's what every McRyan boy wanted to be because that's what their dads and uncles were. However, even as a young boy Mac knew his dad was special. Simon McRyan appeared on the news, was written up in the paper and every tough case seemed to come his way. He was a legend. More than once as a child and then again as a teenager, Mac heard he would have a lot to live up to when he became a cop.

It was assumed, expected, preordained that Mac would walk in his father's footsteps. It was the McRyan way after all. However, even as a fourteen- or fifteen-year-old, Mac was self aware enough to wonder if he really wanted to work under that kind of pressure.

Then another path presented itself.

Mac became a straight A student and stellar athlete at Cretin High School. He was awarded a hockey scholarship to the University of Minnesota where he captained the team to a national championship his senior season as a tough and savvy left wing. He graduated with highest honors from the University and enrolled in law school, with visions of a legal practice and maybe even politics. He graduated summa cum laude from William Mitchell College of Law. Mac accepted an offer for $100,000 a year with a prominent Minneapolis law firm. He was married to his college sweetheart, who also went to law school, graduated with honors and had a similar job lined up with a prominent law firm. They were set for a life of prosperity and success.

But then, as it so often does, life gets in the way and changes the course you have selected.

Mac's two best friends were his cousins Peter and Tommy, both of whom followed the family tradition. They became cops. Two weeks before Mac was set to be licensed as a lawyer, Tommy and Peter were killed in the line of duty.

For most people, they would have taken it as a sign that they made the right choice, to do something other than being a cop. Mac had better options, safer options, more lucrative and socially accept-able options. But the deaths of his cousins hit Mac differently. He didn't want to run from it, he didn't want to feel fortunate, he no longer wanted the more lucrative and socially acceptable option. He didn't feel entitled to it, not when he looked at what the people most important in his life, his family, were doing. Instead, he felt an obliga-tion, to his cousins, to his family and to himself.

A week later he joined the St. Paul Police Department.

Life had veered to a different path.

Now, a short four years later, Mac was about to walk under the crime scene tape for the first time as a detective. He knew his dad would be looking down on him.

Their crime scene was an alley in the middle of a block of one-hundred-year-old brown and red brick buildings. Lich pulled the car to the curb just short of the alley which was now taped off. They each took one last long sip of the hot coffee and then jumped out into the cool twenty-degree March morning as the sun worked its way up on the blue crystal clear eastern horizon.

Lich dropped his dark brown fedora on his round balding head. The fedora, trench coat, suit and shoes were all in shades of Lich's trademark weathered brown. The clothes tightly, too tightly, formed around the bulbous mid-section of his five-foot-eight body. Lich's ensemble made Mac look GQ in comparison. Mac was sporting a black wool trench coat, gray scarf, navy blue suit, light blue dress shirt and blue, yellow and cream striped tie all of which hung comfortably on his blond haired blue eyed six-foot-one athletic frame.

Mac was curious as to how things would go with "Dick Lick." Mac had known him for years, even back when his dad was alive. Lich had the reputation of being a good detective, when he was interested in being one. Good instincts, a nice line of b.s. when needed and the willingness to occasionally think outside the box, little of which had been on recent display. As of late, he'd been finalizing his second divorce and it seemed as if his interest in police work had waned considerably. Given what the McRyan name meant in the department, Mac half-wondered if he'd been assigned to Lich as a way to motivate Dick. Mac would soon find out.

McRyan stepped under the yellow tape and stopped, taking in the scene. The alley was narrow, like a canyon, running between the four- and five-story brick buildings that dotted either side. Dumpsters, the odd car or truck, stray paper, cardboard coffee cups, soda cans, and small dirty snow piles and patches of ice framed either side of the alley. Occasional splotches of graffiti added a certain off-color ambience to the alley. The dumpsters provided an aromatic stench that permeated the air. Garbage pick-up couldn't come soon enough.

"Lovely," Lich grumbled.

The crime scene was a hundred feet ahead. A Ford F-150 was parked along the left side of the alley, the front end nosed at a leftward angle towards the grimy alley wall just past a large overflowing rusty green wheeled dumpster. The coroner was examining a body stuffed into the truck's rear bed and Ramsey County crime scene techs were buzzing around the scene placing small yellow numbered tents to mark potential pieces of evidence, snapping pictures and taking video.

"Your first case, Mac. Why don't you go ahead and run it," Lich offered.

"Are you sure?" Mac asked, a control freak by nature. He definitely wanted the reins.

"Yeah. I've got your back if we get stuck."

Mac nodded, pulled on rubber gloves, opened his notebook and approached the coroner, an old family friend named Jack Coonan. Coonan felt them approaching, looked up, saw Mac and smiled, taking in the young detective approaching him. "Let me see the shield, boy."

Mac pulled his trench and suit coat back to show his shield on his belt.

Coonan smiled. "Is this your first case?"

"First case, Jack. So what do we have?"

"Gordon Andrew Oliver," Coonan answered, handing a wallet to Mac. "Patrol cop ran the plate on this truck and it belongs to Oliver. Bartender also confirmed it was his truck."

"Cause of death?" Lich asked.

"Preliminary is blunt force trauma to the right temple area," Coonan pointed with his pen to the temple area and a large hematoma. Then Coonan pointed to the back right of the victim's head. "He might have been hit first in the back of his head. See the bruising and blood here at the base of his skull?" The coroner pointed with his pen at the right side of the back of the victim's skull. Mac nodded.

Coonan continued: "He might have been hit from behind, falls and hits the bumper with the front right of his head and then falls to the ground."

Mac leaned down to look at the back of the skull, "He was hit more than once?"

"That indeed appears to be the case," Coonan answered. "I'll have to see for sure when I examine him but it looks like he was hit back here twice, maybe three times. I can confirm once I get the body on the slab. But it's the blow to the temple on the bumper that probably killed him. This is very preliminary, of course, but I bet I'll find temporal bleeding and without immediate medical attention, the blow to the front of the head from the bumper was fatal." The coroner was an old pro who didn't idly speculate. Mac suspected much of what Coonan was surmising would turn out to be the case.

Lich was standing to the left of the truck. "So our guy was hit from behind, hits the bumper and falls over here to the left of the truck."

Mac walked over to the left side of the car. He looked at the corner of the metal bumper on the left side of the truck and the smudges of blood on the bumper. In addition to that blood, Crime Scene had also marked the blood pool on the ground, just to the left of the back left side of the truck. There was also a small amount of splatter on the truck's back left quarter panel.

"You think robbery, Mac?" Lich asked, testing.

Mac shook his head, "If it were, why not take the wallet? Jack, was any money in the wallet?"

"Yeah, Mac, couple of hundred bucks, American Express and Discover cards too, plus the guy has an Omega watch, pretty nice, still on his wrist."

Mac looked to Lich, "If you were robbing the guy..."

"...You'd take the wallet, the money and credit cards."

"And you wouldn't stuff the guy in the rear bed of the truck. You'd take the wallet, watch, maybe even the truck, and get out of Dodge."

"So probably not a robbery then. I'm with you so far Mac," Lich said.

"Jack, can you give me a time of death?" Mac asked.

"I'd say somewhere between midnight and two a.m." Mac nodded and jotted down some notes.

"Who found the vic?" Lich asked.

"Bartender from The Mahogany," Coonan answered. "He's talking to the uniform cop back there." Coonan was pointing to the back entrance to The Mahogany thirty feet behind them.

Mac and Lich walked back to the uniform cop who was standing next to a tall, thin, disheveled man with a goatee. They introduced themselves to the clearly shaken bartender named Chet Remer. "You know our victim?" Mac asked.

Remer nodded then said, "Gordy was a regular with us. He was in two or three nights a week, occasionally on a weekend."

"When did you see him last?"

"Last night. He was in like usual after work."

"Where does he work?" Lich asked.

"At a law firm. Krueger, Ballantine, Montague and Preston."

Lich looked to Mac, the lawyer turned cop. "Do you know the firm?"

Mac nodded. "Sure. KBMP is a well-known firm with forty, maybe forty-five attorneys, I think. Their offices are here downtown, over in the old Lowry Lewis Building." Then to the bartender: "Mr. Remer, was Gordon Oliver an attorney there?"

"An associate I think."

"So he was in last night?" Mac asked.

The bartender nodded.

"What time did he arrive?"

"Maybe nine-thirty, give or take. That was kind of a usual time for him. He'd been working some longer hours as of late he said. He said he was gearing up for trial."

"What time did he leave the bar last night?"

"He left around midnight, I think. I remembered he gave me a wave on the way out the back and it was no big deal. He's done it a hundred times I bet."

"Did he always park out back like that?"

"Yeah," Remer answered. "We let a few regulars like Gordy do that. A little perk."

"How was it you found Mr. Oliver this morning then?" Lich asked.

"I went to a little after bar party with some friends last night after we closed at one. My friends dropped me back off at the end of the alley here this morning a little before five. My Jeep is parked back here. I noticed Gordy's truck was still here which I thought was odd since I saw him leave, and leave alone. I walked over and saw the blood on the driver's side. I looked inside the truck's cab, didn't see him and then got a sick feeling in my stomach. So I called 911. The police got here a few minutes later, popped the truck's rear bed gate and flip cover and," Remer's lip started to tremble, "there he was."

"I know this is difficult," Mac said, "but can you think of anyone that would want to hurt Mr. Oliver?"

"No I can't," Remer answered. "He was a good guy, especially for a lawyer."

Mac and Lich both snorted, which Remer noted.

"I know, I know," Remer said. "Lawyers can be a little full of themselves."

"Tell me about it," Lich retorted, looking right at Mac with a toothless smile.

"Whatever," Mac shot back, shaking his head.

Remer picked up on it, "You a lawyer or something?" he asked Mac. "Or *maybe* you're married to one."

"Good pick-up," Mac answered, remembering that bartenders spend significant amounts of time observing and evaluating people. "I was going to be, but then I didn't. Wife is a lawyer."

Remer nodded. "Then you know this is a lawyer bar, right?"

Mac nodded. He'd been in a half-dozen times over the years with his wife and law school classmates.

"Well, we obviously see lots of them in here and, I don't care how much they spend, some of them are real assholes, arrogant and full of self-importance. But Gordy wasn't. He was plenty confident for sure, but he was friendly and not a bad looking guy at all. He dressed well and looked the lawyer part, pinstripe suits, nice ties, fancy watch, spent some money on the haircut, all that. He cut a good look and from what I observed, he had an effective line of bullshit for the ladies."

"Get himself a fair amount of tail, did he?" Lich asked, his mind drifting to one of the few topics he liked to discuss in detail and, as Mac had learned, with great frequency.

Remer smiled. "Gordy left with company plenty of nights. I asked him his secret and he'd just say 'you gotta use all the tools in the toolbox, Chet.'"

"He was killed outside your bar," Mac said, getting back on track. "Did anyone in here give him trouble last night?"

"Not last night."

"How about other nights then?" Mac followed, catching the bartender's drift.

"Maybe a month ago he got into it pretty good with a guy in the bar. It was heated. We had a couple of off duty cops in here that night and they broke it up before it got physical, but it looked like it could have easily escalated to that level."

"Do you know why?"

Remer smiled. "Like I said, Gordy was good with the ladies and from what I saw he didn't really let a diamond ring stand in his way. He almost viewed it as a challenge. I think that night we might have had an angry husband or boyfriend."

"Do you have a name?" Mac asked, jotting down notes.

"I don't. I can check but I don't think we wrote anything up on it."

"Did you recognize the guy?"

"Not at the time. I probably would if I saw him again because of what happened that night. But he wasn't a regular, that's for sure, but whether that was the only time he was in here I don't know. I know he hasn't been back and Gordy never mentioned it again. I think he was here with some people from his law firm that night so they might know more about it."

"Speaking of his work, did he ever mention any trouble there?" Mac inquired.

"No. He worked long hours at that firm like most young lawyers do, but he really seemed to like it. Sometimes he came here with people from the firm, lawyers, secretaries and stuff. I think he was a little *friendly* with a couple of women from the firm or at least it sure seemed like it. But again, he never mentioned any work trouble. He just worked a lot, I know that."

Lich and Mac spent a few more minutes interviewing Remer and then left him and walked back into the alley to look over the crime scene again. Mac walked back to the blood pool and knelt down to look around when a flash of light to his right caught his eye. Under the front of the left rear tire he saw a small brass plate, maybe an inch by half inch, rectangular in shape. It wasn't marked as evidence. Mac pulled a small flashlight out of his pocket. He carefully moved around the blood pool and crouched down close to the brass piece and shined his flashlight on it. It looked like there was blood on it. Mac called over a crime scene tech to mark, photograph and bag it.

Mac stood up and then looked back towards the dumpster and stared for a minute. Lich noticed the look.

"What are you thinking, Mac?"

Mac stood up and walked over to the dumpster and crouched down behind it, careful not to touch the dumpster. There was a gap between the back of the dumpster and the wall. He could peek through and see the back door to The Mahogany. The victim still had his wallet, watch and the car was still there.

"Jack, did the vic have his cell phone?"

Coonan shook his head. "Yes."

This wasn't a robbery, Mac thought. Robber wouldn't put the body in the truck, not to mention the fact that the wallet, watch, cell phone and perhaps even the truck would be gone. Mac peeked back through the opening again. "I think our killer crouched down behind the dumpster here, lying in wait for Mr. Oliver. When Oliver passes," Mac stood up and swung down with his right hand, "the first hit knocks Oliver into the bumper of the truck here. Who knows, there's a patch of ice here as well so after he's hit, he stumbles, maybe steps on the patch of ice and then hits his head on the bumper. Then the killer hits him a time or two when he falls to the ground, finishing off what was already probably a finished job because the blow to the head on the bumper is what kills him."

"With what?" Lich asked. "Hits him with what?"

"I don't know with what yet," Mac answered. "There's the small brass plate our tech is bagging right now that has blood on it, so it might have fallen off of the murder weapon when the killer was swinging it and hitting Oliver with it."

"So what are you thinking, rook?" Lich asked.

"This wasn't random. Someone knew Gordon Oliver was here and knew his truck would be parked back here. He was killed by someone who knew him."

2

"BUT A HOMICIDE IS DIFFERENT, SOMEONE HAS BEEN MURDERED."

While on a long drive for a hunting trip when he was perhaps fourteen or fifteen, unsure if being a cop was what he wanted in life, Mac McRyan asked his dad how he delivered the news to a family that they had lost a loved one. Simon McRyan was a gregarious, outgoing, larger than life personality who knew how to fill a room with fun and laughter. He could make a funny quip about anything and often, when making a serious point, he would start off with some humorous anecdote to soften the impending lesson. However, for this question from his son, Simon McRyan sat in silence for a number of minutes, looking out the windshield, deep in thought, before he carefully answered the question.

Mac's dad quietly said that before he ever informed the next of kin, he always tried to put himself in the shoes of the family and how they would want to be told the news and what they would want to hear from the policeman that was giving them the news. The most important thing was to make an investment in the victim. Then his father looked him straight in the eye and said: "Son, this is the most important thing. If you become a cop, if you work homicides, you speak for the dead. That is the job. You become their voice. That is the obligation and it is a heavy one. It is an obligation that not everyone can carry. If you become a cop and you become a detective and you want to work homicides, you will have to ask yourself if you can carry that burden. If you can, then you can talk to the family because then you have that investment in the case. You will say: 'I'm sorry for your loss,' and it will mean something to the family. They will trust that you will do everything you can to solve it and give them an answer, closure and maybe even a sense of justice."

Mac thought about those words all the way back to the station. The ride allowed him to clear his mind before he made the call; the phone call that changes everything for a family. Lich had managed to find out that Gordon Oliver was from Wichita, Kansas. His father had died two years ago but he was survived by his mother. She was about to hear the news that she'd lost another man in her life. To make matters worse, Mac would have to deliver the news over the phone which didn't seem right but was unavoidable.

He did the best he could with Janice Oliver.

Mrs. Oliver hadn't spoken with her son in a week, other than via a few e-mails. Her son hadn't mentioned any problems with anyone at work or anyplace else for that matter. He enjoyed his work and seemed happy. Mrs. Oliver didn't have any information that seemed helpful. Mac told her he would be in touch with more information as it developed and that she should call him if she thought of anything. He took down a list of other family members to contact. After he hung up, he sat in his desk chair for a minute to collect himself. It had been a difficult conversation.

Lich had been sitting at his own desk twenty feet away, keeping a respectful distance while he listened in. When Mac hung up, Lich left his desk for the breakroom. He came back with a cup of coffee for himself and his partner and said, "All in all, Mac, you did pretty well there."

"Thanks."

"It's different than when you're on patrol. In those cases, it was an accident, right?"

Mac nodded.

Lich continued, "In those cases, it's an unfortunate set of circumstances, and the victim has *died*. It was an accident. But a homicide is different, someone has been *murdered*. It was intentional. The victim is still dead, but a homicide, that just hits people differently. It makes them ask *why?*"

Mac looked down for a moment and then pushed himself out of his desk chair, "Then let's go figure out *why* Gordon Oliver was murdered."

Their first stop was Gordon Oliver's condo, which was a lofted apartment on the far eastern edge of downtown St. Paul, an area called Lowertown. The building, called The Parker Lofts, was a converted warehouse that was subdivided into condos. Oliver had a second floor unit. Mac and Lich, along with two crime scene techs, were let into the unit by the building manager.

The building was a secure building, requiring a key to get in. The front entrance to the apartment, as well as its parking garage, was monitored by video cameras. The manager said he would pull the camera footage to see if anyone unusual entered the building, particularly after midnight.

The loft was approximately one thousand square feet. The floor plan was open, with a kitchen opening into a large open living area that contained a leather sectional couch and easy chair situated around a large area rug and glass rectangular coffee table. The furniture framed a viewing area for the fireplace and a flat screen television. The bedroom and bathroom were positioned down a narrow hallway that ran behind the kitchen.

There was a standard amount of disorganization that evidenced it was occupied by a single, young professional male who worked long hours. The wool blanket on the couch wasn't folded, there were four different bowls and three glasses in the kitchen sink, there were four pairs of shoes, three dress and one tennis, strewn on the floor mat by the door. The bed in the bedroom was unmade, his toiletries were spread across the vanity in the bathroom and papers were strewn across the small dining table near the kitchen.

"The place looks disorganized, but it doesn't look like anyone ransacked the place," Lich observed.

"No it doesn't, although we need to review the video footage from the front door and garage to be sure," Mac answered and jotted down a reminder. He perused the loose papers on the small table, a combination of work papers, legal briefs and cases and a few bills, one for cable and another for his cell phone. A red toolbox sat just to the side of the table and Mac smiled, thinking of the bartender's statement, "You gotta use all the tools in the toolbox." Of course, that referred to Oliver's penchant to chase skirts.

Mac and Lich spent time knocking on a few doors but none of Oliver's neighbors heard anything or were aware of any problems.

"YOU CAN'T MAKE THAT SHIT UP."

The Lowry Lewis Building was a five-story classic located in the middle of downtown St. Paul, six blocks from The Mahogany. The interior of the building featured a five-story courtyard with skylight. The offices opened to balconies that overlooked the courtyard. Marble, carved mahogany and oak were the distinctive finishes of the interior of the historic building. The first floor was occupied by a series of small businesses including a jeweler, shoe repair shop, clothier and barber. Krueger, Ballantine, Montague and Preston occupied the second through fifth floors. The receptionist area for the law firm sat at the top of a wide grand staircase that rose majestically to the second floor from the street level entrance.

McRyan looked at the listing of attorney names on the wall behind the receptionist and counted forty-six attorneys. He recalled from his law school days of interviewing with firms that KBMP, as it was known, specialized in corporate transactions and the complex litigation that attached itself to that kind of work. It was an old-time St. Paul law firm, having first opened its doors as Krueger and Ballantine in 1922. Krueger and Ballantine had long since passed, and Montague was listed as retired. The only name partner still active was

Marie Preston, who was listed as the firm's managing partner. She was who Mac asked to see.

Marie Preston was a woman in her mid-to-late fifties. She wore dark round tortoise shell glasses. Her black hair, with strands of gray, was pulled back in a tight bun. She was dressed in a plain black pant suit, red blouse with a double strand of pearls around her neck. She wasn't dressed matronly but certainly conservatively. Mac broke the news to Preston about Gordon Oliver's death.

"It is such a shock. I saw him here just last night. Do you know who killed him?" Preston said after a few minutes, having regained her composure, although her eyes still watered.

"We're trying to figure that out, ma'am," Mac answered. "What can you tell us about him?"

Preston explained that Oliver was a fourth year associate who was an up and coming litigator. He was an extremely hard worker who had billed over 2,100 hours the previous year and was ahead of that pace in the current year. Good numbers for a young associate, requiring late nights and lots of weekend time.

"Gordon was a good young trial lawyer. He tried his first jury trial last year and won. He had the mindset for litigation, he was going to be a good one, a very good one. A lawyer's lawyer," Preston explained. "He liked the battle and grind of it and he had just the right amount of arrogance for it."

"Arrogance?" Lich asked.

"If you want to be a good lawyer, particularly a good trial lawyer," Mac answered, "you need to be confident. You need to be arrogant."

"And Gordon didn't lack for either quality," Preston added.

"Arrogance, huh. You were going to be a trial lawyer, weren't you, Mac?" Lich said smiling.

Mac shook his head, 'walked right into that one,' he thought. Then to Preston, "You said he worked long hours?"

"If you want to be a good litigator, a good young lawyer for that matter, you must be willing to grind it out hour-by-hour, day-after-day. Gordon could do that and seemed to *like* doing it."

"We're going to have to ask this question of a lot of people around here, but did he have any problems with anyone?"

"Professionally? No. His conduct as a *lawyer* was exemplary. In fact, even though he was a very young lawyer, he'd become something of our professional responsibility expert when others had some ethical questions. Professionally, he was an absolute stickler for the rules."

"But personally?" Lich followed, picking up Preston's tone.

Preston sat back and picked her next words carefully, "With litigators like Gordon, you want them kind of living on the edge, to have something of a fearless attitude, to be willing to go at a hundred miles an hour. They are more effective that way. Gordon was no exception. With those kinds of lawyers you take the good with the bad."

"I assume the good was the legal work and billings," Mac said.

"Yes," Preston replied. "Partners make money on profitable associates. Gordon Oliver made us money."

"What's the bad?"

"Well," Preston answered slyly, "Gordon could be pretty abrasive and well, he *really* liked the ladies."

"So we've been told," Lich said. "At least about the ladies. The abrasive part is new."

"So what about his liking the ladies was a problem?" Mac asked.

"That he shared his affections with *soooo* many of them around the office," Preston replied disapprovingly.

"So many? Like how many?" Mac asked, pen at the ready.

"Well there were at least three women that I know he slept with. There was a secretary, a paralegal and then one of our associates."

"Three? At least that you know of?" Mac asked skeptically, jotting down notes. "Were there more?"

"I suspect there could have been but there are only three that I know of for sure."

"Hey, at least he's equal opportunity, hitting everyone on the law firm food chain," Lich said lightly.

"Indeed," Preston answered. "Gordon was, what one of my fellow partners likes to call, a hound. In any event, the problem in one case was that the woman was married and in another case, the woman was in a long-term relationship and it created some issues, particularly with the married woman."

"What kind of issues?"

"Well, about a month ago we had a rather angry husband appear at our reception desk demanding to see Gordon."

"What was his name?"

"Martin Burrows. His wife Tammy Burrows is a secretary in our office."

"Did Mr. Burrows see Mr. Oliver?" Lich asked.

"He did, unfortunately," Preston related that as Burrows waited at the reception desk, Oliver and two other associates walked up the staircase, returning from a Starbucks run. Burrows attacked Oliver, landing one punch before the two other associates were able to get between them. Building security was called and Burrows was physically escorted out of the building.

"Were any charges filed?" Mac asked.

"No. Gordon let it slide. He didn't want to make it any bigger a deal than it was. Perhaps he should have."

"The bartender at The Mahogany said that Oliver and another man got into it one night at the bar. No blows, but it got heated. Do you know if that was Burrows as well?" Dick asked.

"It might have been. I heard some gossip about that incident but I didn't hear that Burrows was attached to it. Who knows, it might have been the significant other of some other woman Gordon bedded. He was pretty adept at making that happen."

"You mentioned abrasive, how is that an issue?" McRyan asked.

"You know that whole confident, arrogant thing. It rubs some people the wrong way. Some people were put off by his confidence. Partners have been feeding him a lot of work, especially Stan Busch, and Gordon wasn't afraid to flaunt that."

"How about his work? Was there anything he was working on lately that could have caused him some trouble? A difficult client perhaps? Maybe opposing counsel he had an issue with?"

Preston shook her head, "For the last three or four months he's been heavily involved in a case that was supposed to go to trial starting next week. It's a complex shareholder lawsuit. Gordon Oliver was working with another very good senior associate named Michael Harris. Both of them were working for Happy Hour."

"Happy Hour?" Lich asked quizzically.

"Happy Hour is Stan Busch," Preston replied. "I guess he's kind of what I would call our morale partner. He's notorious for taking people out for drinks after work. He's done it for years. We call him Happy Hour."

"We'll need to talk to him and the whole firm," Lich said.

"We'll need a whole roster of your employees," Mac added. "We need to speak with everyone and know who is here and who is not."

"Please wait here for a minute," Preston replied. "I need to make an announcement."

Mac and Lich spent the next three hours interviewing lawyers throughout the offices. The atmosphere was somber. Doors were closed. Discussions were in hushed murmurs. There were enough teary eyes and sad faces to suggest Oliver was liked by a fair number of people around the firm.

They started with the lawyer Oliver was doing most of his work with. Mac and Lich caught Stan Busch a/k/a "Happy Hour" as they exited the conference room with Marie Preston. Busch was just arriving in the office, carrying two briefcases, a black leather litigation case and a weathered tan executive briefcase. Preston informed him of the news.

Busch shook his head, "I knew the womanizing would get him sooner or later."

Mac and Lich shared a look and then followed Busch back to his well-appointed corner office. It reeked of old school lawyer and law firm, with fifteen-foot-high ceilings, crown molding, oak wood floors and dark cherry wood furniture. The office was a power office and Busch looked plenty comfortable sitting in it even given the circumstances. The veteran lawyer was nattily attired in a navy blue pinstripe suit, red silk tie and a crisply pressed blue dress shirt with a white collar. Busch sat casually, one leg crossed over the other, in his high backed leather chair behind his large cherry wood desk, cutting the look of a lord over his law practice.

Behind Busch was a large cherry wood credenza full of family photos, many taken on family ski, beach and tourist trips. Mac could make out two of the pictures which were clearly from Venice. The walls of the office were dotted with pictures of Busch with the powerful and elite of the state; governors, legislators, lawyers and even the odd celebrity. To the right of the credenza, on the floor, were two more high-end leather square litigation cases to which Busch had added the two briefcases he brought with him to the office.

"I like your tan briefcase," Mac said. "Reminds me of the one an uncle bought for me when I graduated law school."

"Thank you," the lawyer responded, glancing briefly to the brief-case and then back to McRyan with a quizzical look. "If you went to law school, why are you a homicide detective?"

"It's a long story. Besides, we're not interested in my story, we're interested in yours and that of Gordon Oliver."

Stan Busch liked Gordon Oliver. "It will be a real loss. He was a very fine young lawyer. Everything you want in a young associate. He was really coming along nicely and I could envision him doing my work and the firm's work for many years to come."

"So we understand Gordon Oliver was working a lot for you as of late," Lich said.

"Exclusively for the last four months. We have a case scheduled to go to trial starting next Monday. Gordon, along with Michael Harris, was going to be covering much of that trial, along with me of course. Gordon was going to handle a number of witnesses at trial. After we are done meeting here, Michael and I will have to start working on a continuance."

"Was he having any trouble with anyone here in the office or on that case?"

"On the case, no. It's a complex albeit garden variety shareholder dispute case. Other than the typical push and pull of litigation, there have been no problems. So no, work was not a problem for Gordon, not at all. My clients really liked him and he did good, very good work, work beyond what most fourth year associates are capable of. Now his personal life? That is another story. *That* will likely provide you with your killer."

"How so?" Mac asked.

Busch shrugged. "I'm sure you've heard. Gordon liked the ladies. I saw him in action a number of times. He used to say, man's gotta use all the tools..."

"...in his toolbox," Mac finished the phrase for Busch. "I've heard that a few times today," Mac added, a tinge of disgust in his voice.

"Gordon said it at least once a day, whether he was doing legal work or chasing the ladies. It was his signature catch phrase, I guess. You'll find it on a wood plate on his office desk."

"So who from Mr. Oliver's personal life would have it in for him?" Lich asked.

"I think there is a husband or two of our female staff that are not fans of Gordon. I'm sure Marie Preston told you of the incident in the lobby a month or so ago."

Mac and Lich nodded.

"Well that wasn't the only time he had to deal with Mr. Burrows. Gordon told me there were phone calls, e-mails and one threat to kill him, so I'd check on that Burrows fellow."

"Did Oliver report the threats to the police?"

"I'm not sure. I recommended he do so."

Mac made a note to look into Burrows the minute they left the firm. "Any other spouses or boyfriends we should look into?"

Busch nodded and quietly said, "You will want to talk to Genevieve Mathis, a paralegal, and Heidi Sawyer, an associate here in our office. I know Genevieve is engaged to be married and Heidi has a long-time boyfriend and I know for a fact that Gordon slept with both of them."

"How do you know this?" Lich asked.

"I saw him leave with them on different nights when we were out at The Mahogany. From what I could tell, they weren't one time occurrences either." Busch gave them the details as best he could recall.

"Sorry I have to ask this, but where were you last night between midnight and two a.m.?" Mac asked.

"No problem detective, I understand," Busch replied reasonably. "I left the office around 6:30 last night and spent the night working at home. I went to bed around 10:30 or so. My daughter stayed the night with me."

Mac and Lich spent another five minutes with follow-up questions and then Mac asked: "So I understand they call you Happy Hour?"

Busch smiled, "Detective McRyan, we demand our people work hard around here, especially our associates, and they make the partners a lot of money. So I don't think it's asking too much to take our people out a few times a week for a drink, some appetizers, an occasional nice dinner at Kincaid's to say thanks for a job well done."

Mac and Lich worked their ways through the offices for the next two hours, interviewing staff and lawyers regarding Gordon Oliver. They took a break in a conference room just after the lunch hour to look at their notes to review who they'd interviewed, who was left and what they'd learned. It was an interesting mix of people to say the least.

"How about that one lawyer, the older guy with the comb-over, what was his name, Sander Anthony, what a piece of work."

"The guy who remembered interviewing me when I was in law school?" Mac asked, taking a sip of coffee. "The one who didn't really like Oliver?"

"Yeah, that guy. He was kind of a douche bag. What did he say about Oliver's office philandering?"

"Wouldn't a *prudent* lawyer avoid the chance of such office scandal by not bedding the help," Mac replied, mocking Anthony's stuffy voice. "The one that cracked me up was the woman lawyer, that little pit bull named…"

"Oh yeah, Powers, Barbara Powers," Lich finished. "Man, she went off on Oliver about his litigation skills, how he did this wrong or that wrong. How cocky and condescending he was."

"Yeah," Mac answered. "She's the one on crack, I think, or at least that's what some others in the office seem to think."

"Why do you say that?"

"As we were walking down the hall I heard a couple of lawyers quietly chuckling about 'Barbie Law.'"

"Barbie Law?"

"Yeah, the gist being she makes the law up as she goes along. Let's just say these folks didn't hold her legal acumen in high regard," Mac said with a wry smile and took a last sip of his coffee. "So let's go over the list. We have some people left to interview. The first one we should interview is Michael Harris, he should be back now."

Michael Harris was a senior associate who worked exclusively with Stan Busch and had worked with Gordon Oliver extensively over the last four months. Whereas Busch's and several other partners' offices spoke of status in the classic building, Harris's spoke of a busy lawyer gearing up for trial. Red rope files were scattered around the floor of his office. Piles of neatly stacked papers created a skyline across his desk and credenza with multicolored cardboard and ceramic coffee cups littered among the stacks. Harris's suit coat was draped over one of his guest chairs. His white button down collar shirt was open at the collar, his plain black tie loose and askew and his shirtsleeves were rolled up to his elbows. No pictures, no art nor even his law degree were to be found on the walls. Harris looked like one of those over-worked lawyers you saw on a television show. Harris was all business.

If others in the firm were surprised by Oliver's death, Harris was the opposite, "I can't say that I'm surprised."

"Why not?" Mac asked.

"Gordy lived on the edge. He worked hard and played even harder."

"How did he play hard?" Lich asked.

Harris looked at Lich skeptically, "Really? How many people have you spoken with around here?"

Mac scanned his notes, there were too many to count, "Let's just say lots."

"And you talked to Happy Hour, right?"

Mac nodded.

"Then you know about Gordon. He was a womanizer, a twenty-four seven hard-on unlike anyone I've ever seen. He worked all day, went out drinking at night with the express goal of getting some action. That included women here in the office and outside the office. He wasn't terribly discriminating." Harris proceeded to give them the women Busch, Preston and others had given them.

"We're going to be looking into that," Mac said. "Were there any other issues, beyond his womanizing, perhaps with work? Was there a conflict with another lawyer or client perhaps?"

Harris shook his head, "This case is really the first one I've worked extensively on with Gordon so I can't be sure but I doubt it. He did exceptional work for me and Happy Hour. He was always available for his clients, almost too available."

"What do mean too available?"

"Oh nothing really. It's just that Gordon would walk around the office with his cell phone attached to his ear. He'd answer it anywhere and everywhere and he would walk around the office talking to clients on it almost as a way to... I don't know... show everyone else," Harris rolled his eyes, "how hard he was working. As if we all weren't. It was all just a little too haughty for my taste."

"You sound like you didn't like Oliver," Lich said, not a question, but a statement.

Harris shook his head. "Gordon was a little annoying and arrogant, that cell phone thing being an example and I certainly didn't approve of his off hours activities and I will not be surprised if that is what ultimately got him killed. But when it came to work, he was all business. I could give him something and he would get it done, done right and efficiently. He was a fourth year associate but he was really doing the work of a fifth or sixth year associate. Gordon was that good. Whatever led to his death, I seriously doubt it had anything to do with how he practiced law."

"Where were you between midnight and two a.m. last night?"

"I left the office at 11:30 and was at my apartment on Grand Avenue within ten minutes and five minutes after that I was in bed and a minute after that I was asleep."

Genevieve Mathis was short, almost tiny, maybe not even five feet tall. She was dressed in a conservative plain black pant suit and cream blouse buttoned at the neck. She had applied a light layer of makeup and her shoulder length straight black hair was generally un-styled unless you counted that she pulled it behind her ears. She had the look of a serious worker in the office and she didn't strike Mac as the type to indiscriminately hook up with someone like Gordon Oliver. She just didn't look the part but the phrase 'you can't judge a book by its cover' jumped into his head as he quickly assessed her. Mathis was a paralegal who worked for the firm's trusts and estates group.

Mac got right to it, "We understand you had a relationship with Gordon Oliver and that caused some issues on your domestic front."

"It wasn't a relationship, detective. I slept with Gordon a few times."

"Why?"

"What does that matter?"

"Mr. Oliver is dead. So it matters," Mac pressed.

Mathis nodded and exhaled, "I have a boyfriend, detective. We've dated for a really long time. I don't know, maybe it got boring and Gordon came onto me a few times. We were out for drinks one night with a small group here from the firm. He asked me if I wanted company. And I surprised myself and said yes."

"When was this?"

"A month ago, the first time was on February 18th."

"Were there other times?"

"There were three times."

"Why only three times?" Lich asked.

"Because I ended it after that. I realized Gordon was sleeping with others here in the office and I felt I was about to become a punch line."

"Did your boyfriend find out about it?"

"I don't think so. I never told him and I really hope he doesn't."

"Why?"

"Because I think he is going to propose."

"How do you know that?"

"I picked up his gym bag the other day and the zipper was open. Everything fell out and one of the things that fell out was a felt ring box. I didn't look inside but..."

"...You think that's what it is."

She nodded. "What I did with Gordon was fun, a guilty pleasure perhaps, but also a huge mistake. I haven't been with a lot of men and he was really good looking and I have to admit the sex was pretty hot. He knew what he was doing and I'll freely admit I enjoyed it, but it was wrong."

"So where were you last night between midnight and two a.m.?"

"I was at my apartment with my boyfriend. It's a secured building with video cameras. I'm sure it will show you the time I came home and that neither I nor my boyfriend left."

One look at Cassidy Burrows told Mac that Oliver didn't have a type, other than she had to be a woman and willing. Whereas Genevieve Mathis was the antithesis of look at me, Cassidy Burrows was all about that. She was dressed less than conservatively with a short thigh high pink skirt revealing her thin legs and a plunging neck line that displayed her ample topside. Mac looked to his right at his partner, who appeared to be undressing Burrows in his own right. Mac gave him a dirty look.

"It's been a long day," Lich growled as he sat back and let his eyes drift elsewhere.

Burrows knew why she was in the conference room and didn't beat around the Busch, taking Mac and Lich aback with her bluntness: "Do you think my husband killed Gordon?"

"Why don't you tell us?" Mac said. "Do you know where he was last night between midnight and two a.m.?"

"I don't know, he moved out two weeks ago," Burrows answered. "But I wouldn't be surprised."

"Is it because of what happened between you and Gordon Oliver?" Lich inquired.

"That's certainly part of it." Burrows related that her husband was moody and temperamental to begin with and it only got worse when he drank. He also had a criminal record.

"Criminal record, what did he do?"

"Bar fight. A long time ago. He nearly killed a guy."

"Why?"

"The way the guy looked at me."

Mac and Lich shared a look. Mac continued, "So knowing this about your husband, that he beat a guy to a pulp for looking at you wrong at a bar, you nevertheless slept with Gordon Oliver?"

Burrows shrugged. "Gordon Oliver was merely a symptom of the problems I had in my marriage. My husband and I haven't been happy together for a long time. At least I haven't been and if he were honest with himself he would admit the same. At some point I realized my marriage was over and Gordon Oliver was a good looking guy who was available, interested and there were no strings attached. I don't regret it in the least."

"How long did you and Oliver sleep together?" Mac asked.

"We didn't sleep detective, we had sex."

Mac shook his head, "Right. How long then, or rather perhaps, how often did you and Mr. Oliver get together for sex?"

"Over a two-month period, probably a dozen or so times. It would be a night here and there. Once in his pickup truck. There were a couple of nooners at the Holiday Inn off of 94 east of downtown. Gordon was a good lay and I liked it."

"Your husband came after Oliver pretty good," Mac said. "Confronting him here at the firm, at The Mahogany, even threatened to kill him once from what we hear."

"That's all true." Burrows related what she knew about the confrontation at The Mahogany as well as when her husband called Gordon at three in the morning threatening to kill him. "That's when I told him to get out," Burrows said. "I haven't spoken to him in a week and haven't seen him in two, so I have no idea where he was last night."

"Where were you last night between midnight and two a.m.?"

"I was with a friend."

"What kind of friend?" Lich asked and Mac snorted, knowing exactly where his own sex crazed partner was going.

"A man, Alexander Burrows. I spent the night at his place."

"Burrows?" Mac asked. "This wouldn't happen to be a relation to your husband?"

"His younger brother."

"H... h... his younger brother, I... see," Mac was in disbelief. He needed a few seconds to compose himself. "Soooo... let me get this straight. Your alibi is that you were sleeping with your husband's younger brother?"

"It is," Cassidy Burrows wasn't the least bit embarrassed or apologetic.

Mac pinched the bridge of his nose and Lich turned away, doing everything he could to avoid laughing. Mac steered into safer territory, taking down information about where Burrows's husband worked, where he was living and where they were likely to find him. They both cautioned her to not contact her husband.

After Burrows left the room, Lich said to Mac: "Did we *really* just sit through that?"

"You can't make that shit up," Mac said shaking his head. "She is a piece of work."

"I'd say if Martin Burrows didn't kill Gordon Oliver, he might kill his brother," Lich cracked.

"Or her," Mac said. "And I'm not sure I could blame him."

"What do you think?" Lich asked as they got ready to leave the conference room. "Does Martin Burrows look good for this?"

"I think we need to be careful."

"Why?"

"Because Burrows looks exactly that, but that's almost too easy."

"What's wrong with easy, I love easy," Lich quipped.

Mac snorted. "You have to love easy. I mean, look at your suit."

4

"THIS WILL NOT END WELL FOR YOU!"

Having finished at the law firm, at least for now, Mac and Lich stopped into the Department of Public Safety to check in with their captain. After briefing him on the status of the case and their one good suspect, they pulled information on Martin Burrows.

Five years ago Martin Burrows spent six months in jail for his role in a bar fight. Apparently Burrows started the fight as his wife had said. He went in with fists and when his combatant answered with a stiletto knife, Burrows broke the end off of a beer bottle and stabbed the man in the abdomen. The man lived and had brandished the knife which apparently had served to mitigate Burrows's sentence.

A review of Burrows's license information revealed he was six foot three, two hundred twenty pounds. His DMV photo gave the appearance of a man not to be trifled with. His square head sat on a neck that looked like a tree trunk. Burrows wore his hair high and tight with a small thin beard sculpted around his mouth. His brown eyes glared menacingly out of the picture. "I think we'll want a little backup when we go see this guy," Mac cautioned.

Mac's cell phone buzzed and it was Jack Coonan. He spoke to Coonan for a moment and hung up. Mac jotted down some notes.

"So what's the Doc have to say?" Lich asked.

"He says his initial assessment at the scene looks correct. The contusion to Oliver's temple is what killed him. The contusion led to temporal bleeding. Like Coonan said, without immediate medical treatment, the wound was fatal. But that's not what was interesting."

"What was?"

"You remember the contusion on the back of his head?"

"Yeah, on the back right side," Dick answered, grabbing the spot on the back right of his head.

"Exactly," Mac replied. "Coonan says the wound to the back of the head was made by a descending blow by someone taller."

"How can he tell?"

"The shape of the wound is like an indentation, made by something that is a half inch wide. The downward angle of the wound suggests that whatever was used came from a high angle from someone taller than Oliver. Coonan thinks the person was over six feet, at least six-two."

"And Martin Burrows is how tall?"

"Six-three."

In the late afternoon, with the sun quickly fading in the west, Mac and Lich tried to find Burrows at the apartment he was renting just off Snelling Avenue near the Minnesota State Fair Grounds. There was no answer to their door knocking. The manager let them into the apartment, which was a small one bedroom. A quick look revealed Burrows was not there. His pickup truck was not in the parking lot either. His wife said that if he wasn't at his apartment, he often liked to ride a bar stool at Drew's Saloon, a small working man's bar on Dale Street, just north of Interstate 694.

Drew's Saloon was a corner bar that occupied half of an old two-story brown brick building with Vittolo's, an Italian restaurant, occupying the other side that fronted Dale Street. They were separate establishments. Behind the saloon and restaurant was a shared parking lot, which Mac cruised. Burrows's red Chevy Silverado was among the twelve vehicles scattered about what looked to be thirty parking slots.

"He's here," Lich said as Mac pulled the Crown Vic into an open parking spot. Mac checked his watch, 6:09 p.m. The sun was just a glimmer in the western sky. It would be dark in a matter of minutes.

"Where's our backup?" Lich wondered.

"Right there," Mac answered with a smile as a patrol car pulled up to the curb running along the parking lot. McRyan jumped out and quickly walked over to the squad car. One of the patrol cops was Mac's cousin Shawn, who powered down his window, smiled and greeted his cousin: "Look at you in the *suit*," Shawn needled as he exchanged knuckles with Mac. "So what do you need from us, cuz?"

Mac gave Shawn and his partner, Victor Montonez, a picture of and the rundown on Burrows, including size, criminal record and general volatility. "So he might be trouble, boys. Lich and I will go in the back. You and Victor stroll in the front and hopefully the show of force will make him come nice and easy."

Mac and Lich allowed Shawn a minute to pull around the front and then casually made their way through the back door. Once inside the back door, they walked down a narrow, inclined, ten-foot hallway into the bar proper. Inside the bar, there was a distinct walkway down the middle to the front door. To their left were a series of booths running the length of the wall to the front window where Mac could make out Saloon in reverse stenciled in cursive on the front window. To their right was the bar, which ran the length of the wall with a break in the middle with an opening that led into Vittolo's. The gap into Vittolo's caught Mac by surprise. He didn't think there was a connection between the two establishments.

"I don't like where he's sitting," Mac whispered to Lich.

Martin Burrows was sitting on a stool next to the throughway into the restaurant. He was carrying on a conversation with two other men and had his back to Mac and Lich. However, he was facing the front entrance and Mac could see his shoulder muscles tense up when his cousin Shawn and Montonez walked in the front door. The patrol cops locked in on Burrows immediately who stepped away from his bar stool and turned to the back of the bar and saw Mac and Lich.

Mac had his right hand holding his suit coat back to reveal his service weapon and his badge on his belt. He held his left hand up, "Martin Burrows, I'm detective McRyan with the St. Paul Police Department. I need to talk to you."

Mac locked in on Burrows's eyes. Burrows peeked to his left, into the opening into Vittolo's. Mac didn't have anyone covering that way and he could tell from the look on Burrows's face that he knew it too. "Martin, stay calm. Don't do something stupid," Mac warned.

Burrows bolted.

"Ahh shit, that's something stupid," Mac muttered as he gave chase into Vittolo's, his cousin falling in behind him.

Burrows was out the front door of the restaurant and burst into the rush hour traffic on Dale Street, just barely avoiding a collision with a Grand Am coming north on Dale and then dodging between a Camry and Dodge Ram pick-up truck traveling south. Mac was out the front door two seconds later. He held his left hand out to halt traffic coming north while Shawn did the same with southbound traffic, leaving them a lane across Dale. Montonez and Lich jumped into the patrol car.

Across Dale, Mac burst ahead of Shawn and gave chase after Burrows, who was twenty-five yards ahead of them running down the sidewalk. Free from dodging cars, Mac quickly closed the gap on Burrows, cutting down ten yards in one block. Burrows crossed another street and then, sensing Mac was closing in, looked back, saw that he was and veered hard right into a narrow alley. When Mac reached the entry to the alley, he slowed some and carefully turned the corner, looking for an ambush.

There was no ambush.

Instead, Burrows was running up the alley, dumping garbage cans, fifteen yards ahead now.

"Burrows!" Mac yelled as he sprinted forward, easily dodging and hurdling the dumped cans, sirens getting closer. "Burrows, stop!" Mac yelled as he quickly closed the gap on Burrows. "This will not end well for you!"

Mac was within five yards now, halfway up the alley. Burrows knew it and moved right and grabbed a two-foot-long two-by-four lying by a garbage can, turned and started to swing it. Mac, anticipating the blow, went in low and put his shoulder into Burrows's midsection, tackling him off his feet before he could finish his swing.

Mac rolled him quickly onto his stomach, put his right knee into Burrows's back, and grabbed his left arm. Shawn, who'd been trailing behind, reached the scene and slapped a cuff on the right wrist and then the left.

Burrows looked like a tied up calf.

Mac, the effort of the two-block sprint catching up to him, looked Burrows in the eye and mocked, between deep breaths, "What were you thinking... running... like that? Do... Do.... Do I look like I'm out of... shape... to you?"

Burrows coughed and spit, "No."

"That's right," Mac answered sarcastically. "I ran the Twin Cities marathon last fall. You were not going to get away from me. Only someone guilty of *murder* would do something that stupid."

Burrows eyes popped out of his head, "Oh my God. Did I really kill him?"

5

"PREDATORS."

It took him three hours to alibi out on the murder of Gordon Oliver. Five minutes of interviewing him, forty-five minutes to get a video file e-mailed from Mystic Lake Casino and another two hours to review the video. Between midnight and two a.m. Martin Burrows sat on a stool at a blackjack table at the casino in Prior Lake, a suburb twenty miles southwest of Minneapolis, a good half-hour drive from the site of Gordon Oliver's murder.

Martin Burrows wasn't their guy.

Nonetheless, for Martin Burrows it was the good, the bad and the ugly.

The good news for Burrows was that he had an iron-clad alibi for Gordon Oliver's murder.

The bad news, as best Mac could tell, Burrows lost at least three hundred dollars. According to security at the casino, Burrows accused the dealer of cheating him and confronted him in the casino parking lot. That confrontation was broken up by casino security.

The ugly was that the Prior Lake police were looking for Burrows because he followed the blackjack dealer from the casino to his apartment and beat him, and beat him badly, in the parking lot.

Burrows thought he'd killed the dealer when Mac accused him of murder.

As Mac scrolled through the video to confirm the alibi, things got interesting at 2:45 a.m. when Burrows was clearly getting agitated, standing and pointing at the dealer. At 3:07 a.m., Burrows looked to have lost eighty dollars on a hand he'd doubled down on. He slammed down his chips and pointed at the dealer again. This brought security to the table and Burrows was escorted out of the casino. The dealer's shift ended at 5:00 a.m. Apparently Burrows waited in the parking lot and followed the dealer to his apartment in Prior Lake and beat him badly. The dealer was alive and in stable condition at the hospital.

Burrows ran because he thought Mac and Company were there to arrest him for the beat down on the dealer. He knew nothing about the murder of Gordon Oliver.

Once in the interrogation room and when Mac and Lich were certain that Burrows's alibi would hold, the man broke down. His marriage was falling apart, his hours were way down at his job and everything seemed to be spiraling out of control. Mac felt some sympathy for him.

The Prior Lake police would be stopping by to pick up Burrows for his pending legal issues in Scott County. Before they did, Mac took a moment with him, sitting on the edge of the table, next to Burrows's chair: "Martin, you've got some anger issues, dude. Going after Oliver, threatening to kill him, all that. I know he was sleeping with your wife and your marriage is falling apart, but I gotta tell you, I met your wife today. She's definitely not worth throwing your life away over. You're a young guy and you've got a lot of years left. Now you're going to do some time for what you did to that dealer, and you should. The man will make it but you did some damage. While you're doing your time, get yourself some help. Maybe have your attorney make some anger management counseling part of whatever sentence you end up with. Because if you don't get that temper of yours under control, the next time you lose it you might end up killing someone and you will have thrown your life away."

~

It was a few minutes after ten when Mac and Lich strolled into McRyan's Pub, the other McRyan family business. The two grabbed stools at the bar and were served Grain Belt Premiums by a retired detective now bartender. Mac took a long pull from the bottle and exhaled and looked at his watch. He had a meeting in an hour a few miles away.

"So your first case, what do you think so far?" Lich asked, taking a pull from his beer.

"I'm thinking we spent the day interviewing and talking to a lot of people and our one good lead went in the shitter an hour ago," Mac replied with disgust.

"Happens," Lich replied lightly, having seen it a hundred times.

"I've been thinking though," Mac said, taking another drink. "Oliver seems to have had two things in his life, his job at the law firm and chasing skirts. He did those two things and that seems to be it."

"What's that tell you?" Lich asked.

"That we'll find our murderer out of one of those two things. It's either something he's been working on or..."

"...someone he's been working on," Lich said. "He's working a case or he's workin' a broad."

"That's right, workin' a broad," Mac said, shaking his head, a perturbed look on his face.

"What?" Lich said, seeing the look.

"I hate guys like Oliver."

"Womanizers?"

"Predators. I've known guys like him for years. Played hockey with them, went to college and law school with them. I've seen friend's wives and girlfriends pursued by guys like Gordon Oliver. They like women in relationships. They like to pursue them. They like the challenge of it."

"It's like Charlie Sheen," Lich said.

"How so?" Mac asked.

"He said he paid for prostitutes, not because he wanted them to stay but because he wanted them to leave. It's the same thing here. Oliver gets the married woman. She's not going to stay. It's like Cassidy Burrows said. No strings attached."

Mac disagreed. He turned and faced Lich. "Dick. That doesn't make it right."

"I'm not saying it does," Lich answered defensively.

"You're not exactly disapproving," Mac retorted and took a long drink of his beer. "It's just flat out wrong. It can ruin peoples' lives. Look at that Mathis woman at the law firm. She wouldn't have pursued Oliver. But he pursued her like it was a conquest. That could have ruined a relationship that she'd been in for years. Same thing with Cassidy Burrows. He was acting without thinking about any of the consequences attached to those actions."

"Is that why you gave Burrows that pep talk back at the station? Because of Gordon Oliver?"

Mac shrugged. "I don't know. The guy has issues but his remorse seemed genuine. I suspect he's going to have plenty of time to think about what he did and I thought it couldn't hurt to encourage him to get some help, that's all."

"Ah, that catholic upbringing is showing through, lad. Father Flynn at the Cathedral would be proud of you, boyo," Lich said in his best Irish brogue.

Mac checked his watch, took one last sip of his beer and dropped a ten on the bar.

"Time for one more?" Lich asked. "I'll buy."

Mac shook his head, "I've got to make one more stop before I go home."

6

"THE QUESTION NOW IS HOW MUCH DO YOU REALLY WANT TO KNOW?"

Mac met Meredith Hillary at a hockey party his junior year at the University of Minnesota. Mac was excelling on the ice for the Golden Gophers, playing on the second line, starting to see power play time, playing a physical and fearless brand of hockey that made him a huge fan favorite at Mariucci Arena. He was certain to be voted captain at the end of the season. He was a big man on campus, knew it, strutted around like one and enjoyed the benefits of it.

Meredith Hillary was impossible to miss at the party. She was hauntingly attractive with dark green eyes, a bright smile with long legs to match her long black wavy hair. And she was smart, studying to go to law school, which Mac had been giving thought to as well. Mac had a new girlfriend at the time but Meredith was unattached and once she met him, she pursued him and it didn't take long for Mac to let her catch him. He was in love and thought she was too.

Meredith came from money. Her father was a senior executive at General Mills and her mother was a renowned vascular surgeon. They both made their way up from humble beginnings and now enjoyed the fruits of their labor and the status they had attained. Meredith was bound and determined to do the same. She wanted the professional success and the status that would come with it; the wealth, the big house, the fancy cars, the beautiful children who went to expensive private schools and colleges. She wanted the good life and she wanted the trophy husband to go with it.

Michael McKenzie "Mac" McRyan seemed to fit the bill perfectly.

He wasn't going pro as a hockey player but he was handsome, ambitious, smart if not borderline brilliant, graduating magna from the University of Minnesota and heading to law school. They married after their second year of law school together. Mac had a six-figure job lined up post law school which meshed well with her similar job offer from a large firm.

Mac was happily on board with the plan that Meredith had set in motion.

Then his two cousins, his two best friends, the co-best men at his wedding, were murdered in the line of duty. Mac felt the calling of the family business and changed the plan.

Meredith was not on board.

She didn't want him to do it. She didn't understand why he needed to do it. In her mind, Mac should have felt just the opposite. He should have felt fortunate that he could avoid such a dangerous line of work, blessed that he had options in life that were more lucrative, safe and in her mind acceptable. She said he was destined for more than working a police beat.

Mac couldn't give in, wouldn't give in to her on this one. He had to do it. There were four generations of cops in his family. He had numerous uncles and cousins who were cops. He idolized them, worshipped them and until a few years before, had always wanted to be one of them. His two best friends had sacrificed their lives. Their sacrifice left Mac feeling like what he'd done in life, no matter the success he'd had, no matter the money he'd make or the status he would attain, would ever match up. It would never come close to what his family had sacrificed, to what Peter and Tommy had given. This was something he had to do as a man, as a McRyan, and Meredith needed to realize this. It hadn't been part of the master plan but life has a way of intervening and changing your course. It wouldn't have to be forever but for a time, so that he could look his family in the eye.

This was vital to him. He simply had to do it. He wanted the woman he loved on board. He expected the woman he loved to be on board.

Meredith either didn't understand it or simply viewed what Mac was doing as beneath him and, by extension, her. He upset her carefully crafted plan and she was not happy with the course change. She married a lawyer who at a minimum would become wealthy and at a maximum, could become much more. She didn't set out to marry a cop. A few weeks after he got out of the academy and was working patrol, Mac overheard Meredith talking to her mom, derisively saying "he'll do this for a few years, get bored and will realize he is wasting his talents. Hopefully he'll realize it before it's too late."

Mac never confronted her about it but it motivated him all the more. Proving her wrong and showing her that he was right became his motivation. He wanted to prove to her that this was the right thing for him, that they could have the life she envisioned, maybe just getting there a different way. He was out of a uniform and with the vice squad within two years. He worked some undercover for another year and became a detective within four years before he reached age thirty. Mac was on his way. And it wasn't just on the job, but financially as well. He'd also invested in the Grand Brew Coffee shops. That little ten grand investment was paying off twenty fold and was certain to provide more.

Yet Meredith was unhappy.

Things had changed.

There was no going back.

The last six months Meredith came home later and later at night. There were a few nights where she said she was working through the night and just stopped home in the morning to shower and change clothes. A new case came up that required trips to New York, Washington and San Francisco. She became distant at home. Their love life, once extremely active and adventurous had essentially come to a halt.

At first, Mac wanted to believe it was just that she was as driven to succeed in her career as he was in his. But he had always taken pride in being brutally honest with himself and knew he was in denial. All the telltale signs were there. He was virtually certain of it but he needed to be sure.

Mac knew five retired cops who became private detectives. The best of the lot was John Biggs, a detective who once worked cases with and had the respect of Simon McRyan. Biggs ran a small private investigation firm and developed a very good reputation and catered to an exclusive clientele. Three weeks ago Mac hired Biggs to find out if his instincts were right.

At 11:00 p.m. sharp, Biggs let Mac into his office. A thick manila folder with Meredith Hillary McRyan written on the tab sat in the middle of Biggs's desk along with a bottle of Johnny Walker Black and two glasses and that told Mac all he needed to know.

"Looks like I was right."

Biggs walked behind his desk and took the cap off the Scotch and poured two fingers in each glass. "I'm sorry, kid," Biggs answered simply as he handed Mac a glass. "The question now is how much do you really want to know?"

"Everything."

"You sure?"

Mac simply nodded. In his heart and his head he knew this was the case and was mentally prepared for it. Nevertheless, the reality of it still hit him like a punch to the gut.

"Take a seat."

Biggs flipped open the folder. He had two clipped sets of pictures, handing one to Mac. Biggs or one of his investigators followed Meredith Monday through Friday up until three days ago, when Biggs had seen enough and began to put together his investigative report. Biggs walked through the report and pictures with Mac. Biggs was good, very good, Mac realized objectively. He had the goods. He caught Meredith in the act on multiple occasions.

It was with whom that threw Mac.

Meredith worked on complex corporate litigation and many cases would involve five or six attorneys, usually a senior partner, a junior partner and three to four associates. Mac had figured Meredith found another similar aged associate at her law firm given she was working late and traveling more on firm business. But that was not the case and who she was sleeping with told him everything he needed to know about his wife, what he was blind to about her all along. Their relationship was less about love and more about social status. When Mac was at the University and in law school he looked like a man who was on the right path. He was on the path of status, wealth and notoriety. These were the things, Mac realized, that mattered most to his wife. Meredith was more concerned with status, wealth and looks than love and honor. She had to be because she was having an affair with the senior partner she'd worked with since she first joined the firm, the very married forty-seven year old J. Frederick Sterling.

"Surprised it's Sterling?" Biggs asked.

"Stunned."

"Me too," Biggs answered. "Because I did a little research about his marital history."

"Which told you what?"

"Well, J. Fred here is on his second marriage," Biggs answered. "And he has a prenuptial agreement with the current Mrs. Sterling that has an *interesting* provision or two."

"Interesting?" Mac asked, catching Biggs's tone. "Interesting how?"

"If they divorce she gets $350,000 and that's it." Biggs took a drink of his Scotch.

"Pocket change for a guy with his money," Mac answered with a dismissive wave. "From what Meredith told me a few years ago, he's worth at least seven or eight million dollars."

Biggs held up his hand, "Except there's an infidelity clause in that prenup my friend. If they divorce because he's caught *cheating*, she gets a cool five million."

Mac's jaw dropped, "Five million... dollars." Mac whistled. "Really?"

Biggs nodded with a satisfied look on his face.

"Hmpf. I'm surprised you didn't run into a private investigator tailing him. She ought to have one on retainer just to protect herself."

"I seriously thought the same thing but we didn't see anyone," Biggs said as he lifted the bottle and Mac nodded. Biggs poured more liquor into Mac's glass. "A friend of a friend of an acquaintance got me a look at the prenup. Apparently the first marriage went tits up because J. Freddy was schtuppin' wife numero dos."

"So wife number two knows that Sterling has the wandering eye and writes in a little protection," Mac adds. "He stays faithful or if not..."

"It'll cost him," Biggs finished. "The language is rock solid, if he gets caught cheating, he owes the five million. Of course that would be on top of the rather sizable monthly alimony of $25,000 he pays to wife number one from his first divorce eight years ago, not to mention child support for three kids at Blake School, which runs him somewhere in the neighborhood of eighty grand a year. Now he took home a little under $900,000 last year so he's not living check to check—yet. If he gets divorced because he gets caught with his fly down, it'll cost him dearly."

Mac's strategy and terms for divorce suddenly became crystal clear.

7

"SO WHAT IS THIS THEN?"

Mac got home at 1:15 a.m. Meredith was already asleep and given what he'd just learned from Biggs, couldn't bring himself to join her in bed so he simply racked out on the couch. Never one who needed more than a few hours of sleep, he was up by 5:30 and went for a long run.

When Mac decided to become a cop, one thing he agreed to was buying a house. The house, of course, needed to meet Meredith's expectations. Consequently, the house was most definitely at the upper end, and in reality, beyond what they probably could afford at the time, a 4,500 square foot Victorian in the Mac-Groveland neighborhood, four blocks east of the University of St. Thomas. While he never had any formal training, Mac was handy with tools and interior design. He'd spent the better part of the last four years on various restoration projects in the home, including the furniture layout and color scheme. It was plenty livable when he started but it was now a beautiful home and would, if he put it on the market, easily net him double the original purchase price, even in the flat-lined real estate market. That day was soon coming, but until then Mac would enjoy another of the house's perks, its close location to Summit Avenue.

Summit Avenue ran east from the Mississippi River a little over four miles to downtown St. Paul. It was a boulevard filled with stately mansions, synagogues and churches, majestic one-hundred-year-old trees, the Minnesota Governor's mansion, his law school William Mitchell College of Law, the University of St. Thomas and Macalester College. It was a wonderful stretch of city for a morning run.

He put his earphones in, set the music to random and began his run in the cool March air. The morning jogs were always important to him. He worked problems out in his mind in the solitude of the early morning. For the last several months, he'd thought through his marital issues. Now he had a plan for dealing with that. This morning he wanted to think about something else, the Gordon Oliver murder. His first case and after one day, he felt stymied.

The first thing he did was mentally run through everything he knew. For the next twenty minutes he ran through the crime scene. Oliver had been hit from behind on the back of his head, but there was no weapon at the scene that they could find. While he hadn't seen the final autopsy report, Coonan was sure the weapon used was not something like a tire iron or something else heavy. It was enough with the force of the blow to knock him down, but not enough to kill him. The blow to the front of his head on the bumper had taken care of that. The weapon was not found at the scene so the killer dumped it elsewhere or, while unlikely, still had it. Mac had noted the small brass plate with blood on it. It might have come from the murder weapon although it could have just as likely been lying on the ground and Oliver fell on it and that's how his blood ended up on it.

Forensics might be able to shed some light on what the killer hit Oliver with. The forensics report would probably be in his e-mail inbox when he got to the Department of Public Safety. Oliver's truck had been dusted for prints on the outside. The only prints found belonged to Oliver. March nights were still cold in Minnesota and the killer probably wore winter gloves so prints were unlikely.

He crossed Dale Street, three miles into his run. Mac ran the Twin Cities Marathon the previous fall. The last stretch of the marathon was along Summit Avenue. Since training for the marathon, he'd kept running five days a week. He checked his sport watch and he was running at a steady seven minute pace.

The murder just didn't feel random. It wasn't a robbery. His money and credit cards weren't missing. Oliver's Omega watch and cell phone were still with him. How about a briefcase? Mac hadn't thought of that and made a mental note to see if perhaps some legal papers were missing. Perhaps that would give them a lead.

It likely wasn't a robbery because the body was placed in the back of the truck. Were it a robbery, the money, watch, cell phone and anything else of value would have been taken and the killer would have left the body. They wouldn't have taken the time to hide the body. But why did the killer feel the need to hide the body? They wanted a delay in it being found perhaps? They needed the time to set up their alibi? Mac could almost sense in his mind that the murder was a split second decision made by the killer and then an 'Oh shit' moment and the killer puts the body in the truck and ditches the scene as quickly as possible.

That strongly suggested it was someone who knew him.

Mac reached the St. Paul Cathedral, the halfway mark of his run and pulled out his cell phone. He had some good thoughts and quickly sent an e-mail to his work computer before he forgot them. He played random music on the first stretch of his run but Mac wanted some Springsteen for the return run and selected *Darkness on the Edge of Town*. Mac checked his watch and started the run back towards home.

It wasn't random. Therefore, the case would be solved through the people involved in Gordon Oliver's life. The law firm and The Mahogany thus far were the two consistent places in his life. He worked long hours at the law firm. He was at The Mahogany several nights a week. The profile Mac and Lich were developing of Gordon Oliver was a workaholic who blew off the stress of his job with sex, often with women from work or The Mahogany. Those were the 'tools in his toolbox,' Mac muttered to himself.

Martin Burrows, now that would have been nice and easy. Burrows had been perfect but he had an air tight alibi. Perhaps there was another aggrieved husband or boyfriend out there that they had yet to discover. He and Lich would need to re-canvas the bar and the law firm to dig further. Forensics was downloading his home computer and e-mail and Mac wanted to review it to see if anything jumped out at him. They were also working on getting access to his law firm e-mails. The County Attorney's office was working through the issues on that. It wasn't that the law firm was being difficult, just crossing their i's and dotting their t's on their obligation to protect their client's information.

Mac crossed Snelling Avenue at 6:15 a.m. heading west, now in the last stretch of his run. The traffic was starting to pick up some now on Summit Avenue, the morning rush not far off. He made a last mental checklist of what he'd thought about as he kicked it down for his house, finishing the last mile of his eight-mile run at 6:27. He stopped a block short of his house and walked the rest of the way for a cool down, sending himself another e-mail of his thoughts on the case while he did so. They would be in his inbox when he got to work in an hour.

Mac walked up the driveway to the side portico entrance of the house and into the kitchen. He grabbed a bottle of water out of the refrigerator as Meredith walked into the kitchen in a dark olive dress suit and off white blouse and three-inch heels. She looked good. She always looked good.

Mac started a pot of coffee and said, "I was thinking we haven't had a dinner together in a while."

"No we haven't," Meredith replied looking at her watch and waiting for the coffee to finish brewing. "I can't tonight, I'll be working late. This Clanex merger is proving to be a killer."

"I suspect I will be working late tonight as well," Mac answered. "I picked up the Gordon Oliver murder."

"I heard about that yesterday," she answered. "Word is he was probably killed by some jealous husband. I hear he was quite the ladies' man."

"Yeah, women should be careful about men like that," Mac replied, curious if Meredith caught the meaning. "Anyway, how about tomorrow night? I can try to be home by seven. I could pick up some Chinese," which was her favorite. "I've got something I want to talk to you about. It's kind of important."

"I think I can make it," Meredith answered as she poured coffee in her travel mug.

~

At the station, Mac and Lich discussed the case over coffee and came to the conclusion they needed to go back to KBMP and interview everyone again. Mac brought in two additional veteran detectives, Frank 'Double Frank' Franklin and Rick Beckett, as there were upwards of eighty people to go back through. It was a long morning and early afternoon. Mac and Lich re-interviewed everyone from the day before while Franklin and Becket interviewed others in the office that had less exposure to Oliver.

A little after three p.m. they reconvened in a small law firm conference room to review notes. Stan Busch gave Mac and Lich a list of cases that Oliver had worked on for him the past six months. Michael Harris worked on most of the cases with Oliver but recalled nothing about the cases that were a problem.

"Gordon could be extremely combative in depositions, at times overly so," Harris said. "I've seen him piss off opposing counsel and deponents more than once. But that's standard and most of the people we had Gordon depose were usually lesser players in the cases. I tended to handle the bigger fish so I'm hard pressed to think of anyone in a case that would want to kill Gordon. I can't think of one case where that was an issue."

"How about clients?" Mac asked. "Was there ever a client that Oliver had issues with?"

"Not one that I can think of," Harris answered. "Like I said the other day, Gordon was really attentive to our clients and our clients are pretty happy. Stan reels them in and I do the litigation work with Gordon's help, at least until yesterday. Gordon was a pain at times, detective, but like I said yesterday, I'll miss the guy. As a young associate, he was money."

Further interviews with the rest of the firm's lawyers revealed that in the last six months most of Oliver's work was with Stan Busch. There was some real estate litigation that Oliver worked on for Marie Preston and one case for another partner, Jackson Lund. No problems were noted with those cases yet more names were collected to potentially interview.

Franklin and Beckett interviewed the firm's staff and their results reaffirmed one immutable truth of the work place, the staff always knows more about what's going on in the office than the bosses. Turns out that Gordon Oliver had slept with not three, not four, not even five, but six different women in the firm, including one partner. Beckett and Franklin interviewed the law firm's IT manager who said that Gordon told him one time that he had his own little Yahtzee card. It required sleeping with a receptionist, secretary, paralegal, associate and a partner. The staff knew that he'd completed the card by recently bedding a forty-three-year-old partner named Constance Bernier on the leather couch in her office.

"She said 'he got me at just the right time,'" Double Frank said.

"This dude was good," Beckett added.

"He'd fuck a goat if you held it for him," Mac replied disgustedly.

"You saying he had it coming, Mac?" Franklin asked.

"No. I'm merely stating the fact that he was a douche bag when it came to women."

"It's probably what got him killed though," Dick added. "We just have to find the person he pissed off the most and we have our killer."

"How about the other women he slept with?" Mac asked. "Do any of them look good for it? Have boyfriends or husbands who look good for it?"

Franklin and Beckett shook their heads. "Two of the women now have boyfriends although they didn't while they were serving as a love receptacle for Gordo," Beckett said. "They both claim they were home with their new boyfriends last night. We'll follow up but I'd bet my pension they alibi out."

"What about Bernier?" Mac asked.

"She flew in from Atlanta this morning. She was there for the last four days."

"We could look at her financials and see if she hired someone to do it?" Lich speculated.

"We can and should but does this really look like a hit to any of you guys?" Mac answered, shaking his head. "If it were a hit, there would be a bullet in his head or a hitter would have known enough to make it look like a robbery gone bad. He would have taken Oliver's wallet and watch. This looks like neither."

"So what is this then?" Beckett asked.

"This is someone angry at Oliver who made a mistake, didn't mean to kill him or made a split-second decision to kill him for some reason. This person didn't really know what they were doing, panicked and quickly hid the body and ran." This train of thought gave Mac an idea. "Maybe there's a surveillance or security camera that caught our guy nearby?"

Lich was skeptical. "Mac, none of the buildings in the alley had any cameras, at least not ones on the alley."

"I know that," Mac answered, thinking broader. "I'm thinking in the vicinity, within the three or four block area. Maybe we'll get lucky and see someone walking, running or driving away from the area that is tied to Oliver, The Mahogany and the law firm." Mac thought for another minute and looked at Beckett. He was good with video and computers. "Rick, you and Franklin hit the establishments around The Mahogany and get any video running in the time window of the murder. Maybe we'll get a hit off of that."

"What are *you* guys going to do?" Beckett asked, a tinge of bitterness in his voice, knowing how boring surfing hours of video could be.

Mac looked at his watch which said 3:44 p.m. "We're going to go back to the station for a few hours. I want to go over everything we have and then Dick and I are going over and re-canvassing The Mahogany when it starts getting busy. I want to hit it when most of the staff and regulars are around."

8

"IT MUST BE THE LAW FIRM."

Lich said he needed a break before they went over to The Mahogany. Mac was okay with that. It gave him some time alone with the case to work through the evidence. One thing Mac learned from watching his father over the years was that at some point in a case you needed to sit down and take a look at everything and see if a pattern, string or trail developed.

In law school, a professor happened along Mac studying in the law library. He saw Mac had written 'jurisdiction' and drawn a box around it on his legal pad. He had a line to the left that read 'personal jurisdiction' and a line to the right that read 'subject matter jurisdiction,' the two components necessary for a court to have jurisdiction over a particular case. Then notes were jotted around each of the words. The professor smiled and said, "Mr. McRyan, you are mind-mapping."

A mind-map is essentially a diagram that uses words, ideas, tasks or other items arranged around a central key word or idea. Mac saw his father do it when he was a kid. Mac picked it up and used it in college and then law school. He never knew it was called mind-mapping but that's what Professor Becker was telling him and Mac apparently had a good understanding of jurisdiction. He aced the Civil Procedure final.

While Lich took his leave for a few hours, Mac jotted 'Gordon Oliver' in the middle of the page, drew a rectangle around it and started jotting down notes in bullet point format:

- *Associate at KBMP for 4yrs.*
- *A very good young litigator according to several attorneys including Preston, Busch, Bernier, Anthony, Lund and Harris.*
- *Worked killer hours, strictly litigation, going to trial next week.*
- *No problems professionally at work.*
- *Mr. "All the tools in your toolbox." His signature catch-phrase for work and pleasure.*
- *Womanizer. Slept with at least six women at law firm, probably more. 1. Burrows alibi'd out. 2. Mathis home with boyfriend. 3. Bernier in Atlanta. Other women are not good suspects, no apparent motive (might need to evaluate further?).*
- *The Mahogany is favorite bar. Confrontation at bar but it was with Burrows, who alibi'd out.*
- *No other apparent social life beyond law firm and bar.*

Mac drew another line away from Gordon Oliver and jotted down 'Crime Scene' and drew a box around it:

- *Alley at The Mahogany.*
- *Time of Death - Midnight - 2:00 a.m.*
- *Blunt force trauma to temple was the fatal blow.*
- *Not a robbery. Still had wallet, watch and cell phone. New Ford F-150 left behind. If robbery all would have been taken and body left behind.*
- *Body stuffed into truck bed. Why? To hide it. Why hide it?*
- *Hit from behind by someone who was tall, at least 6'2" based on wound angle. Weapon unknown.*

- *Brass plate with blood. Unsure if from murder weapon. Forensics still evaluating.*
- *Why use the alley? If not robbery, then he was killed by someone who knew him. Alley was a good location but killer had to know that he would be there. Only someone who knew him well would know he would be there. The killer knew him - really knew him.*

Mac circled that notation on the legal pad. The killer knew him —*really knew him.* So how many people *really* knew him?

Mac leaned back in his desk chair and twirled his pen in his fingers. Now that was something to think about. Only someone who knew him or talked to him all the time would know he was at the bar that night and at that time. Someone could have followed him or they knew he was there and then could lay in wait.

Mac opened the folder on his desk that contained Oliver's cell phone records. He'd asked that the records identify the number and identity on the other end of the call. A cell phone was essentially one of Oliver's appendages according to the attorneys at his firm. The records reflected that. On the day he was murdered, he had thirty-three cell phone calls. Mac shook his head. A record day for him might be ten calls and this guy had thirty-three. The day he was killed was not an outlier. As best Mac could tell, he averaged some-where around twenty-five calls a day.

As for the day he was killed, the calls appeared to be from a collection of clients and from the firm. A number of calls were identi-fied as being from the clients he was going to trial with next week on the RFX Industries shareholder suit. Opposing counsel in the case must have been from French and Burke as there were three calls from that firm. Gordon had calls from Stan Busch, Michael Harris, Constance Bernier as well as two from his secretary and one from a paralegal. The firm calls were mostly between 11:30 a.m. and 1:30 p.m. and as Mac looked back on his notes, Oliver took a long lunch that day with some other attorneys from the firm. Towards the end of the day, there was one call from Stan Busch at 6:30 p.m. and another from

Michael Harris at 8:22 p.m. Mac made a note to follow-up on those phone calls to see what Harris and Busch discussed.

He had to have been killed by someone who knew him, but why? Could be the womanizing but Mac was starting to think that was not the cause. Martin Burrows was their one good suspect on that angle and he was out. The others just didn't feel right nor did the evidence really point in their direction. Nobody else seemed bitter enough to want to do anything to Oliver.

Mac looked at the crime scene photos and in particular the pictures of Oliver. He had this nagging impression that given how the murder took place, the killer didn't really know what he was doing. It was as if there wasn't a plan. The first blow to the back of Oliver's head was with something strong enough to stun him and knock him over but, according to the coroner's report, it would not have been enough to kill him or even do any real damage beyond stunning him. It was Oliver hitting his head on the bumper that was fatal and that wound appeared to Mac as if it happened by chance or luck or even possibly bad luck. It would have taken real talent to have known that hitting Oliver from behind would have caused him to fall and hit the bumper. If the killer went for revenge, he would have used a tire iron or a bat if the plan was to hit Oliver from behind. Neither the evidence at the crime scene nor the wounds to Gordon Oliver revealed the use of any such weapon. The killer may have brought and, it appeared at this point, probably left with the weapon used to hit Oliver in the back of the head. But in the end, there was a definite lack of viciousness to the murder. It was almost as if it happened by accident.

Mac kept thinking that the killer knew Oliver well. Knew his habits, his routines, where he liked to hang out. The killer knew, had to know, that Gordon Oliver was granted the privilege of parking in the back at The Mahogany. That he would be there, that he would come out the back. Given what they knew of Oliver thus far, it struck him that somehow his murder tied back to the law firm. These were the only people who seemed to know him really well.

"It must be the law firm," Mac muttered.

"Why?" Lich answered. Mac was so engrossed in what he was doing he didn't realize his partner was back.

"How long you been back?"

"About ten minutes or so there, partner. I've just been sitting here watching you. You were so intensely focused I didn't want to interrupt. So why is it the law firm and not some spurned lover or the lover of a spurned lover?"

"I've spent the last two hours running through the case. The angry boyfriend, fiancé or husband theory doesn't add up for me."

"At least not yet," Lich cautioned. "Given how prolific our guy is, I'm sure there is a woman he bedded that we've yet to uncover."

"I'm not dismissing it completely," Mac answered. "There could certainly be someone out there we are not aware of yet. But even with that, I don't buy the angry boyfriend angle anymore."

"Why not? Seems that's the one thing he was doing that pissed people off."

"True."

"So why the firm and not some jilted lover or boyfriend or husband or ex-husband?"

"Because of where he was killed, Dick. He was killed by someone who knew his habits, where he went, when he went there and that he would park his truck behind the bar. At this point, the only people who know Oliver well enough to know those things are the people at the law firm. I'm just thinking it has to be someone there and Oliver knows something, has something on someone, maybe he saw something that made someone need to track him to the alley behind The Mahogany for some reason. We find that, we find our killer."

Lich sat down in the chair next to Mac's desk. "Let's assume you're right, which I'm not completely convinced that you are, but let's say you are. That means going deep, much deeper at the law firm. You may know this better than I but at least in my experience, law firms do not give into something like that willingly."

"No, they'll fight us because it probably means us getting into e-mail, files and all that stuff lawyers and law firms like to claim privilege over although that's a bunch of bullshit," Mac answered derisively, looking at his watch. "Look, it's after six now so we'll have to wait until tomorrow to get with the County Attorney's office to evaluate our more involved access at the law firm. In the meantime, we can go back to Oliver's apartment and see if we missed anything. Then we can cover our bases and go to The Mahogany."

"I can't wait," Lich sighed.

9

"YAHTZEE."

Mac cut the crime scene tape covering the door to Oliver's apartment and he and Lich walked in. Mac carefully dropped a backpack containing a picture camera and video camera on the floor. They both pulled on rubber gloves.

"So what are we looking for?" Dick queried, his arms folded across his chest, looking around the apartment.

"We'll know it when we see it," Mac answered as he walked down the back hallway to the bedroom. When they'd been to Oliver's place the day before, Mac had given only a cursory look to the bedroom. Now he wanted to take a longer look. If Oliver had something to hide, perhaps he'd have hidden it at home and, in the absence of a home office, the most likely place to hide it would be in his bedroom. Mac stood in the doorway, hands on hips, surveying the landscape.

The bedroom was square in shape, probably twelve-by-twelve, with a long walk-in closet in the far right corner, wrapping behind the bathroom in the hallway. The room itself contained a queen-sized bed, walk-in closet and small Ikea three drawer dresser and night-stand. Mac started with the nightstand, which had a drawer resting over two shelves. The drawer contained a box of condoms, a spare watch, two pens and the remote for the small television sitting on top of the dresser. Next he moved to the dresser. The top drawer was the sock drawer, half athletic socks and the other dress socks. Underwear occupied the middle drawer and white t-shirts in the bottom drawer. He searched through all the drawers but all they contained were socks, underwear and t-shirts.

Next was the closet. While dress codes had relaxed at law firms over the years, litigators still needed to be ready to go to court at a moment's notice. Gordon Oliver was clearly ready if that were the case. The man was a suit horse. Mac had recently bought five suits for work to go with the five he already owned. He figured he'd use the suits and sport coats he had to have enough variety in clothes for the job. Oliver had him waxed.

There were eighteen suits, ten sport coats, twenty-five dress shirts and ten pair of shoes. The guy worked long hours, made good money and was unmarried. He spent a good chunk of his disposable income on clothes.

Mac checked the pockets on the suits, coats and pants and didn't find anything of interest. There were three storage boxes on the shelves above the hanger rod. He pulled them down and searched them. One had athletic equipment, spikes, a softball glove, softballs and two baseball hats. Another box contained what looked like law school papers, two appellate briefs for moot court competitions, a series of Oliver's resumes and cover letters.

Mac opened another folder and chuckled. It contained form rejection letters from law firms. It was a rite of passage in law school. Mac and his law school buddies used to hang the rejection letters up on the wall. They all said the same thing. We thank you for your application, your credentials are extremely impressive and you will do well in your legal career—*just not at this law firm.* He put the letters back and moved to the third box which contained personal effects, some photographs and financial information on his law school loans. As he looked through it, Mac didn't find anything of interest.

Mac checked the bathroom quick, looking under the vanity. Other than a box of condoms, spare towels and extra bathroom supplies, there was nothing of interest. Walking back towards the living area, Mac opened the hallway coat closet. Inside he found two trench coats, a ski coat and a brown leather jacket. There were tennis shoes and some additional casual shoes on the floor. A box on the top shelf contained a collection of winter gloves and hats. Leaning in the back corner were his golf clubs and a softball bat. Otherwise there was nothing of interest in the closet.

Lich was looking through the kitchen cabinets when Mac walked back in and sat at the kitchen table. "I didn't find anything in the living room obviously," Dick said. "The kitchen doesn't have anything either. Heck, half the cupboards are empty. Oliver didn't have much in the way plates, glasses, things of that nature."

"Single guy who works all the time, not a surprise," Mac said, looking under the kitchen table. "He didn't care much about how his place looked, smelled or was organized. I mean, he's got this dirty toolbox sitting under the table. I mean, what's he even... need... a toolbox... for?" Mac stared at the box. "Could it be that simple?"

"What?" Lich said, seeing the look on Mac's face.

"You have to use all the tools in the toolbox," Mac mumbled as he flipped the metal clasps loose and opened the toolbox. A dusty tray sat in the top with a few screw drivers, wrenches, tape measure and hammer. Mac pulled the tray out and looked into the box itself. "Huh."

"What?"

Mac pulled out a yellow folder that was clasped closed. "Grab the camera out of my backpack."

Lich walked back to the door into the apartment and grabbed the backpack Mac brought along. Dick pulled out the camera and snapped three photos of the envelope. Mac then opened the top and slid the contents out onto the table. There was a computer flash drive and copies of a death certificate, driver's license and other various papers. Mac read through the documents and a smile crept across his face.

"What do you have?" Lich asked.

"Yahtzee."

10

"YOUR WHOLE LIFE IS A LIE."

A t 10:03 p.m., Mac pushed into the interrogation room with Lich, sat down at the table and looked across at his suspect.

"Why am I here?" Michael Harris asked.

"You tell me, Michael," Mac answered acidly, dropping a stack of paper down on the table in the interrogation room, "Or should I say Jordan. As in Jordan Paris."

You could have knocked Michael Harris a/k/a Jordan Paris over with a feather.

"You look surprised. Wait until you see what *I found*," Mac added with dramatic flair. "You know what they say. You gotta use all the tools in the toolbox."

In Gordon Oliver's toolbox, Mac found a binder clip of documents that showed Michael Harris was in fact Jordan Paris and that the real Michael Harris was dead and had been for eight years. McRyan and Lich spent the better part of the last four hours putting it together.

Jordan Paris, who was now sitting across the table from them, graduated from the University of San Diego School of Law cum laude eight years ago. In his final year of law school, as required in California, he submitted his application to the Committee of Bar Examiners for the State of California. To be admitted as a lawyer in California, the applicant must be shown to be of appropriate moral character for the practice of law. Jordan Paris had a felony drug conviction from his sophomore year in college when he was running with a bad element. A drug sale went sideways, there was gunfire and one person was killed. Paris didn't shoot anyone, was largely in the wrong place at the wrong time, but ended up with six months of jail time and a felony conviction. After his jail stint, Paris re-dedicated himself to his schooling and managed to fight his way into law school. While worried about getting admitted to the California bar, he thought with his clean last four years and good grades, he'd be able to show evidence of reform and rehabilitation. Then in the summer between his second and third year of law school, Paris was arrested for driving while intoxicated. His application was rejected by the committee as he was viewed as lacking the moral character for the practice of law. He filed an appeal, which failed. He would not be admitted to the practice of law in California.

Paris met Michael Harris while in his second year of law school. Harris was attending Thomas Jefferson School of Law in San Diego. The two ran into each other in the law library at the county courthouse. Paris could tell right away, Harris was a loner. Yet they struck up a friendship. When Paris was down on his luck, with no job, even fewer prospects and almost no money, Harris offered him the couch at his apartment. One month later, Michael Harris was killed in a car accident.

At the time of his death, Harris was just starting his own law practice, running it out of a run-down job share office with four other young lawyers. Harris was an only child and both his parents were dead. He appeared to be a loner and few people seemed to notice that he passed. When he died and nobody seemed to be missing him, Jordan Paris made a calculation.

Jordan Paris became Michael Harris, proving the Committee of Bar Examiners for the State of California correct about Paris's lack of moral character.

Paris assumed his friend's identity, moved to Florida and was admitted to the bar. After three years practicing in Florida, he moved to Illinois for two years and then had been at KBMP for the last two years. At KBMP he became the model senior associate, working almost exclusively for Stan Busch, trying cases and putting himself on a potential path to partnership.

Harris impressed Oliver. So much so that Gordon Oliver called a friend of his named Jane Phipp, who worked the career center at the Thomas Jefferson School of Law. Oliver raved to Phipp about Harris, how personable he was and what a good lawyer and mentor he was. Phipp related to Mac that she said to Oliver that she didn't remember Michael Harris in that way and the two of them did a little more talking and corresponding and they realized they were not talking about the same person.

Oliver did what good young lawyers do, research. Mac had to hand it to him. Gordon Oliver pretty much had it all and was dead on based on what Mac and Lich had dug up in the last three hours.

Mac laid it all out on the table for Paris.

"This is not what you think, detective," Paris pleaded. "I did not kill Gordon Oliver."

"I don't know, Jordan," Mac replied casually. "It seems to me like you've got huge motive to have done so. Oliver figures out you're not who you say you are, that you've assumed Michael Harris's identity and that you've been practicing law under his name. He confronts you about it a day or two ago, threatening to expose you to the firm, the authorities and anyone else who would be interested. I mean, you're finished but good. Before he does that, before he reports you, maybe he offers you some sort of alternative. Maybe he's worried about the damage it will do to the firm, so he gives you the chance to come clean or maybe just leave town, a little get out of jail free card. Whatever it was, it doesn't work for you. So you went to The Mahogany to confront him."

"You might not have even wanted to kill him," Lich added.

"That's right," McRyan stated, sitting back in his chair, folding his arms across his chest, his right leg over his left, "You just wanted to talk again, but he rebuffs you. He'll have none of it. Everything is falling apart. So you lose it. You hit him in the back of the head. Gordon stumbles, falls and hits his head on the bumper. Then he isn't moving. He's dead. You killed him."

"So you panic," Dick followed. "You put his body in the back of the truck and you get the heck out of there. It might have helped if you'd grabbed his wallet, watch, etcetera... so that it looked like a robbery. I'm a little surprised you didn't think of that. It certainly caused us to look in other directions, such as the law firm where we found you."

"I didn't kill him, detectives," Paris exclaimed. "I didn't even know Gordon knew about me. If he did, he didn't let on at all. I had no idea."

"Come on," Lich replied exasperated. "You can't expect us to believe that."

"It's true, you have to believe me."

"Why?" McRyan retorted. "There's nothing about you that is true, that is real. Your whole life is a lie."

"That's true. What you say is true, everything, except the part where I killed him," Paris exclaimed and then slumped back in his chair, rubbed his face and exhaled. "Look, I've been pretending to be Michael Harris for eight years. I've grown eyes in the back of my head. I could sense a couple of people might have been on to me in Florida so I moved on. Same thing when I worked in Chicago, there was a lawyer in the office who started asking some questions that told me it was time to get out while I could. So I could smell it coming in Miami and Chicago. But I got nary a whiff here. I had no clue."

It was Mac's turn to sit back. His gut was telling him Paris might be on the level. He looked over to Lich who was unimpressed with Paris' performance.

Mac flipped back through some pages from his notebook. "You said to me the other day that you left your office on the night Oliver was murdered around 11:15 p.m., correct?"

"Yes."

"That's plenty of time for you to get to The Mahogany and to the back alley and wait for Oliver to leave."

"I went right home that night. I left the office at 11:15, I got to my apartment at 11:25 and I was asleep ten minutes later. I was exhausted from preparing for trial."

"Can anyone verify that?"

Paris's head went down and his shoulders slumped. He shook his head. "I live alone. I drove to my apartment along Grand Avenue, parked and went into my place."

"Any security in your building?"

Paris shook his head.

"Any cameras that could verify your arrival?" Mac followed.

Paris shook his head.

"Any neighbors you saw on the way in?" Mac asked.

"No."

"That's not exactly what we would call airtight there, Jordan."

"I don't know what else to say, detective," Paris uttered. "It's the truth."

McRyan and Lich stepped out of the interrogation room and into the hallway. It was after midnight. "So what do you think?" Mac asked.

"I think he's guilty as the day is long," Dick answered. "You *actually* have doubts?"

"I don't know."

Lich rolled his eyes. He was tired. It was late. "What? Something is bothering you, Mac, so frickin' spit it out."

Mac plopped himself down into his desk chair, pinched the bridge of his nose and exhaled. "The part where he says he'd grown eyes in the back of his head. Something about that rang true to me."

Lich grabbed his own desk chair and rolled it over to Mac's desk. He sat down, leaned forward in his chair, his elbows on his knees, ready to impart a little wisdom on his smart but young partner. "Mac, the guy has been lying to people for eight years. He's gotten really good at it. Now I hate admitting this, especially to you, but in my experience lawyers tend to be pretty bright people, Mac. They're smart. Paris adds to that, a well-developed ability *to lie*. Put those two things together and you have yourself a lethal weapon—which is capable of doing who knows what. In this case, the lethal weapon was willing to kill. Mac, he killed Oliver two nights ago. Since then he's had plenty of time to think about what he would say if we got onto him, which we did. He's playing us, he's playing you. Don't let him."

"Maybe you're right," Mac answered as he sat back up to his desk. A forensics report was sitting on the desk. The forensics reports identified where the blood covered brass plate from the crime scene came from. "Or maybe I am right."

"Huh?" Lich said.

Mac handed him the forensics report. "Take a look at what that blood covered brass plate is from."

Dick read the report, and looked up to Mac.

"Do you remember where we saw one of those?"

Lich nodded.

"We got the wrong guy."

11

"I CAN PROVE IT ALL."

Stan Busch sat awaiting Mac and Lich in the interrogation room. Busch, as usual, was smartly attired in a black pin stripe suit, white monogrammed dress shirt and red silk tie, looking like a million bucks. In the last eight hours Mac and Lich managed to reveal that looking like a million dollars and living a million dollar lifestyle was why Stan Busch was their man.

Mac and Lich observed Busch briefly through the mirror into the interrogation room. Assistant Ramsey County Attorney Bobby Young was standing with them. It was easy to see that Busch was angry, upset and also, at least to Mac, nervous. He was conferring with his lawyer, a local legal heavyweight named Saul Tobin. Normally Tobin would be reason to be wary, he was good, very good. However, Mac and Lich had the goods.

"You ready?" Lich asked.

"Let's go," Mac answered, picking up a green garbage bag and leaving the viewing room. The two detectives stormed into the interrogation room.

"Arresting me at the courthouse on some bullshit murder charge in front of my legal colleagues? You two have a lot of explaining to do," Busch started. "Saul and I are going to have your badges."

"Lighten up, Stan, you're gonna wanna hear this," Lich said flatly.

Mac took Dick's lead in: "Let me tell you a little story, Mr. Busch."

"About what?" Busch snorted.

"About why and how you killed Gordon Oliver."

Busch snorted.

"Don't say a word, Stan," Tobin ordered.

"Counselor, he won't have to," Lich responded casually.

"No, he won't," Mac added confidently and then started. "We've done some looking into you, Stan, these last eight hours once it became clear *you* were our guy. For me, I wanted to know why you killed Gordon Oliver. I knew that you did but I needed to know why. And you know what? I think I know."

"Oh, do you now," Busch spit.

"Stan," Tobin warned.

"I do, Mr. Busch, and it's the oldest reason in the book. Money. We looked over your billings for the last three years. You have been billing Michael Harris at $350, $375 and $400 per hour the last three years. He billed 1,922, 1,988 and 2,189 hours in those years. My Cretin High math tells me that's $2,293,800 of billings by Michael Harris on your files. I also know that you recovered 96% on your billings, so there has been very little discounting taking place."

"We also understand," Lich added, "that under your firm's compensation system that you receive significant credit for those billings come bonus time, not to mention your own time that you put on those files. That's why you've made $748,000, $792,000 and $849,000 in the last three years from your firm. Michael Harris has helped make you wealthy."

"So what?" Busch answered.

"So what? Michael Harris isn't a lawyer and you know it," Mac answered, looking at Tobin, who flinched. It was clear that counsel for the defense was unaware of this little tidbit of information. "In fact, you know that Michael Harris's real name is Jordan Paris."

Mac looked over to Tobin. "Counselor, to bring you up to speed, Jordan Paris is a graduate of the University of San Diego School of Law but he was never ever admitted to the practice of law in California or any other jurisdiction because of some criminal issues of his own many years ago. The real Michael Harris, who was Paris's room-mate at one time, is dead as the result of a car accident eight years ago. Paris assumed his identity, moved to Florida, then Illinois and finally here, holding himself out as Michael Harris."

"Of course we don't need to tell you this, Mr. Busch, do we?" Lich added. "Because you already know."

"Indeed you do," Mac continued, flipping through his notes and then turning his attention back to Busch. "We checked your phone records and those of the law schools. You called both the Thomas Jefferson and University of San Diego School of Law in the last week. They remembered you just as they remembered Gordon Oliver calling them about the same thing two weeks ago. Your Michael Harris isn't a lawyer."

Mac looked over to Tobin, "Counselor, if a law firm finds out that one of their lawyers wasn't one, what does the firm have to do with the fees paid for the legal work of the non-lawyer?"

"Disgorge the fees," Tobin answered.

"I thought so," Mac said and then to Busch: "Since Harris, or shall I say Jordan Paris, only worked on your files, that's $2,293,800 in legal fees that would have to be returned. Not to mention all the money you would owe back to your law partners. And the alimony from your marriage, holy cow your financial situation is tanking worse than Enron. And oh-by-the-way, can you imagine the damage such a disclosure would cause to your book of business going forward? There are a lot of lawyers in this town, good lawyers, and that busi-ness would be gone in a blink of an eye and you would be gone from KMBP in the next blink."

"And if that wasn't motive enough, there was your other little ethical issue two years ago. You remember don't you Mr. Busch. That case where you failed to disclose a settlement offer to your client, a settlement offer that was significantly more than what the jury awarded your client at trial," Lich added. "That resulted in complaint to the Office of Lawyers Professional Responsibility, a malpractice claim and some rather bad press for the firm."

"Not to mention the loss of a multi-million dollar client," Mac added. "Given how tenuous that put your position with your firm, you had plenty of reasons for wanting to take care of this problem with Paris before anyone found out."

"That may all be true," Busch answered, "but on the night Oliver was killed I was at home with my sixteen-year-old daughter which I know you have verified. I left the office at 6:20 p.m. and went home and never left until I came into the office the next morning."

"We talked to your daughter yesterday," Mac answered. "She did say you were home when she went to bed at 10:30 or so. She even recalled setting the alarm for your security system before she went to bed and recalled shutting it off the next morning before she left for school."

"Like I said," Busch said confidently.

"So we checked with your security company," Lich responded. "They confirm your daughter's story. But then they also have the system being deactivated at 11:20 p.m. and then re-activated at 12:48 a.m. So why would you have done that?"

"Perhaps my daughter did. I was asleep."

"You're lying. You turned off your security system. You left your house. You went to The Mahogany and killed Gordon Oliver."

Busch laughed it off. "That's a nice story. A nice theory even. But you can't prove any of it."

"I can prove it all," Mac answered as he opened the garbage bag he had brought in and pulled out Busch's weathered tan executive briefcase and slammed it on the table. Next to the briefcase, Mac placed a series of photographs.

"Do you recognize this briefcase?" Mac inquired.

Busch didn't respond but Mac detected a slow leak of air from Busch's posture.

"It's yours. We got it from your office this morning." Mac reached for the first picture which was of Busch leaving the Lowry Lewis Building at 6:22 p.m. on the night of the murder. "As you can see you are leaving the office with this briefcase."

"So what," Busch answered.

Lich slid another picture in front of Busch and his lawyer. This picture was a close-up of the briefcase.

"As you can see, there are two of these small brass plates along the bottom of the briefcase, framed by the vertical stitching running down from the handle," Mac noted and then pointed to the briefcase. "Now today there is only one brass plate on the briefcase. What happened to the other one?"

"You tell me," Busch replied flippantly.

"Fine, I will," Mac quickly replied as Lich placed another picture in front of Busch and his lawyer. It was the crime scene photo of a matching brass plate with blood smeared on it. "We found this at the crime scene. The blood on the brass plate matches that of Gordon Oliver. It also matches the brass plate for your briefcase. You want to know why I'm sure it is?"

Busch didn't respond.

"I know because forensics took your briefcase and found Gordon Oliver's blood on it right where the brass plate would go," Mac pointed to the lower right corner of the briefcase and a small area of discoloration.

"You did a pretty good job of cleaning the blood off the briefcase," Lich noted. "But I would have thought you'd have stumbled onto a CSI episode at some point and have learned that it's really hard to get rid of blood. Even when you think it's gone, it's not."

"You brought this briefcase to the alley behind The Mahogany. You hit Gordon Oliver in the back of his head, which knocked him down, and then hit him twice again. In the process, this brass plate fell off your briefcase," Mac thundered on. "You told me to prove it and I have. To quote Gordon Oliver: 'I've used all the tools in the toolbox.' I've proven you were there, you hit him with your briefcase and you killed him. Stan Busch, you're under arrest for the murder of Gordon Oliver."

Saul Tobin was a good lawyer and knew that his client was guilty. It was only a matter of how long he would spend in jail. The rest of his life or maybe have a few years of freedom at the end of his life.

Fifteen minutes later, McRyan and Lich got a full confession from Busch.

Stan Busch didn't go to The Mahogany intending to kill Oliver. He went hoping that he could buy Gordon Oliver's silence or at least more time to take care of the Harris problem. In the alley, Busch had tried to reason with Gordon Oliver, even offering him $100,000 in cash as a down payment, which he had in the briefcase. Oliver wouldn't give in, said that Busch had to come clean on Harris and if he didn't Oliver would. Busch got upset, walked after Oliver and hit him from behind with the briefcase. The $100,000 in the briefcase made it heavier and the blow to the back of Oliver's head sent him sprawling. Oliver fell and hit his head on the bumper. He looked dead and Busch hit him twice more to be sure and then placed the body in the back of the truck and ran from the scene.

12

"IT'S BLACKMAIL."

M ac pushed his way through the backdoor into his house, a twelve-pack of Grain Belt Premium bottles in one hand and a plastic bag full of Chinese food boxes in the other. Meredith called and was ten minutes away. Mac opened a beer and took a long sip from it. He set the Chinese food boxes out and grabbed a couple of plates. He would wait for her to arrive.

How to handle this situation was something he'd run through his head for the past three hours. He'd considered a myriad of ideas. He'd given some thought to romancing her one last time and then dropping things on her but that didn't feel right. Packing her bags and having them at the door had been another but that didn't feel right either and, given the last two days, he was simply too tired to do it. Instead he opted for the direct approach. This would be a confrontation that ended on his terms.

Meredith pushed through the backdoor looking tired from the day. Her look softened slightly at the beer and Chinese food. "Ah, dinner," she said, sitting down and starting to put some food on her plate.

"More like the Last Supper."

Meredith stopped scooping food and sat back in her chair. "That sounds a little ominous."

"Because it is," Mac answered and slid a manila folder over to her.

Meredith was on guard now as she flipped open the manila envelope. The first picture was one of her walking with Sterling.

She frowned.

The next picture was of the two of them entering a hotel room at the Marquette in Minneapolis.

Her eyes popped open.

The last picture was of her in bed with Sterling.

Her jaw dropped.

"You son of a bitch," she growled.

"That's rich. You're cheating and *I'm* a son of a bitch," Mac growled back.

"What gives you the right...?"

"What gives me the right?" Mac railed in response. "Love and honor? For better or for worse? In sickness and health? Till death do us part? Ring any bells for you there, Meredith?"

"This is your fault, not mine," she answered, pushing away from the table and standing up. "You screwed everything up. This could have been great but you had to go be a cop."

"How shallow are you?" Mac replied angrily. "Don't answer because I now know the answer. But you know when we got married I thought it was for love. I really did. I was in love. I thought you were too. But I was wrong. Instead, at the time I simply met your husband criteria. I've come to realize you're like one of those old Andre Agassi commercials. *Image* is everything."

"Give me a break."

"No, seriously Meredith. It is. You wanted a trophy husband who was good looking, rich with the right career so that you could have some sort of perfect looking life. If love was included, well that would be a nice upgrade but it wasn't required. It was as if picking a husband was like buying a car to you."

"You could have taken some of my desires into consideration

when you made some of your decisions, Mac. The decision to become a cop was not one that *we* made. *You* made it. What I thought didn't matter. If you loved me you would have taken that into consideration. Instead, you just went ahead and did it."

"I had to."

"Oh bullshit," Meredith sneered as she paced around the kitchen. "This whole obligation to your family crap is what has driven us apart."

"You know what I don't get?"

"What?"

"What's been so bad, Meredith? You live in a beautiful home. Was it beautiful when we bought it? Maybe not. But I made it that way. I worked my ass off on it. Do we have money? We do. Sure I don't make what I would have as a lawyer, but my investment in the coffee shops has paid off. Our other investments, which I manage, are doing well. We have plenty of money together and more on the way. What was *so* bad? Why isn't that enough for you? Why wouldn't a loving husband and all that be enough?"

"It's just not. Not for me," she answered. "I had something else in mind when we got together. I envisioned something else and this wasn't it. I don't care what you think of my reasons, Mac. I just don't care anymore. I'm not happy. I want out. I've wanted out for a long time."

"What, so you and J. Frederick Sterling can go and live that life you're looking for?"

"He's unhappy like I am. That's what led to this. We are both unhappy."

"So he's who you want to be with?"

"Yes. I'm sorry but I do."

"He's a two-time loser you know. You'd be wife number three."

"I don't care."

Mac shrugged his shoulders. "Okay then. But I have terms."

"Terms?" Meredith asked quizzically. "We'll just split everything."

"You see, that's not going to work for me," Mac answered, shaking his head. He held up the picture of Meredith and Sterling in bed. "J. Frederick fill you in on his prenup?"

"I know he has one. She gets $350,000 upon the divorce. We've discussed it."

"I bet that was scintillating pillow talk."

"Jealous?" Meredith replied, satisfied with herself.

"*Riiiight*," Mac sneered, "of you and J. Fred. I don't think so. But I do have a question for you."

"Which is what?"

"Has he asked for a divorce yet?"

"No but he's going to."

"Are you sure about that?" Mac asked with a tone that caught her attention. "Do you know about the infidelity clause in his prenuptial agreement?" The look on her face said she didn't. "I didn't think so. If he's busted cheating on his wife he owes her $5,000,000."

Meredith saw where this was going, "You wouldn't dare," she hissed.

Mac snapped his fingers, "Like that. I will not hesitate in the least."

Meredith sat back down and stared daggers at Mac whose expression was emotionless. After a minute, she quietly asked, "What do you want?"

"I want it all. You keep your retirement plan at work and I get everything else including the house, the investments and the Grand Brew ownership interest. That's the deal and it is non-negotiable," Mac answered icily.

"The house? The investments? You take it all?" Meredith asked dumbfounded. "How is that fair?"

"It's not, and I don't give a rip," Mac answered. He had the leverage and intended to use every last bit of it. He had no sympathy for or love left for her at the moment. She had betrayed him, hurt him and he was going to get his pound of flesh. He pulled an envelope out of his backpack addressed to Mrs. Sterling and slid it across the table to Meredith. "My terms or this gets delivered. Your boy will be out five million and he probably won't look so attractive to you at that point nor you to him. You, in *sooooo many ways*, will get screwed over if any of this gets out. I'm already gone, but if this gets out, J. Freddy is gone, your career will be gone, everything. So this is the price you will pay for me to go away quietly." Mac had done the math and on his terms he would come out of the divorce with nearly $500,000 between the house and investments. If Meredith ended up with Sterling after all this she'd be fine. "Agree to my terms and you can have those pictures and they'll never see the light of day."

"It's blackmail."

"Yes it is, counselor." He reached inside his backpack and pulled out another manila folder that he slid across the table to Meredith. It contained a divorce settlement with his terms in writing. "I'll give you twenty-four hours to consider this. But you fuck with me on it and I will burn you at the stake, Meredith. I will do what I say. You know me. You know I will," he said coldly, absolutely no emotion in his voice. "You've got twenty-four hours to look them over." Mac pushed himself up from the table. He grabbed another beer and twisted the top off. "And you have five minutes to get out of *my* house."

A half hour after Meredith left, Lich arrived. In the midst of his second divorce, he was the perfect person to commiserate with. The two detectives sat in front of Mac's big screen in his family room, watching the Minnesota Wild play the Vancouver Canucks. After two periods, the Wild were leading 3-2. It was a good game, with three fights and lots of physical play. Mac was on his ninth beer at this point, every bit on his way to getting obliterated.

"You need another beer?" Lich asked as he pushed himself up off the couch, having finished his.

"Is the Pope catholic?" Mac responded, holding up his empty.

Lich was back in less than a minute with two beers and one of the Chinese food containers.

Mac told Lich everything about what happened, Meredith cheating, hiring Biggs to investigate her, J. Frederick Sterling, the prenup, the showdown with Meredith, everything. Lich just listened and laughed when appropriate and was amazed at how harsh Mac was in demanding terms in the divorce. It helped Mac to vent but in the end he felt sad and empty. "I just can't believe I'm sitting here and all of this happened."

Lich nodded and said, "I hear you, brother."

"What happens next?" Mac asked. "You've been through this, what did you do?"

"Everything wrong," Lich answered.

"How so?"

"After my first marriage broke apart, I immediately started dating again and I was remarried within a year. That marriage lasted five long, agonizingly painful years, Mac. It was a mistake and frankly it has screwed me for the rest of my life financially. I'll be paying through the nose." Lich's second wife was a social worker and made half what he did. Between alimony for her and his first wife, Dick wasn't going to be left with much for himself.

"In retrospect what should you have done?"

Lich took a sip of his beer and then said: "If I had to do it over again, Mac, I'd have taken my time. I would have taken a lot of time. I wouldn't have jumped into anything right away. Men often do that and it ultimately doesn't work well. The first time around I never let myself heal emotionally and I made some bad decisions and here I am again and I gotta tell you, it's pretty tough. I find it hard to push out of bed in the morning sometimes," Lich said, stuffing Chinese food into his cheeks.

"What gets you up in the morning?"

"The job," Lich answered, wiping the corner of his mouth with a napkin. "It's the one thing that I have done well in my life most of the time. I get up and I go to work and I try to help people. Like today, we brought some closure to Gordon Oliver's mother, that's no small thing."

"No, I suppose it's not."

"No it's not. It matters, Mac. What we do matters. It's something that didn't seem to dawn on your wife, or soon to be ex-wife, but what we do makes a difference. And let me tell you one other thing."

"What's that?"

"You're a good cop, Mac. Very good."

"Thanks, partner."

"Don't mention it," Lich responded, taking a big swig of his beer. "When I was assigned to work with you, the captain thought you needed a veteran hand to guide you through the work. From what I've seen, the apple didn't fall far from the Simon McRyan tree. So if I were to impart any guidance on you, it wouldn't be about police work."

"What would it be about?"

"Get healed. Get yourself some casual tail, put some murderers in the can and make a difference. And in time," Lich held his bottle out towards Mac in a toast, "you will find a woman worthy of Michael McKenzie 'Mac' McRyan."

Mac smiled and clinked bottles with Lich, "I'll drink to that."

What to read next...

The St. Paul Conspiracy - McRyan Mystery Series #2 (preview included)

Silenced Girls - FBI Agent Tori Hunter Mystery Series (preview included)

A note to my readers...

Thank you for reading and I sincerely hope you enjoyed *First Case - Murder Alley (novella)*. As an independently published author, I rely on each and every reader to help spread the word. If you enjoyed the book please tell your friends and family and if it isn't too much trouble I would really appreciate a brief rating or a review.

Thanks again and I'm always writing a new book so look for Mac in the next mystery! To stay on top of the new releases and new series please join the list at www.RogerStelljes.com and I'll let you know when the next one comes out.

ALSO BY ROGER STELLJES

MCRYAN MYSTERY SERIES

First Case - Murder Alley

The St. Paul Conspiracy

Deadly Stillwater

Electing To Murder

Fatally Bound

Blood Silence

Next Girl On The List

Fireball

The Tangled Web We Weave

Short Stories

Stakeout - A Case From The Dick Files

Boxsets

First Deadly Conspiracy - Books 1-3

Mysteries Thrillers and Killers - Books 4-6

FBI AGENT TORI HUNTER SERIES

Silenced Girls

To receive new release alerts join the list at

www.RogerStelljes.com

ABOUT THE AUTHOR

Roger Stelljes is the New York Times and USA Today bestselling author of the McRyan Mystery Series and the FBI Agent Hunter Series. He has been the recipient of several awards including: the Midwest Book Awards - Genre Fiction, a Merit Award Winner for Commercial Fiction (MIPA), as well as a Minnesota Book Awards Nominee.

Never miss a new release again, join the new release list at www. RogerStelljes.com

Made in United States
North Haven, CT
20 March 2024

50250250R00050